**Paul Swallows** was born in Sydney in 1970. Raised in country Australia, he has since travelled widely and has a particular passion for Italy.

He works as an accountant, based from an office at home; and enjoys cycling, good food and drink, and (of course!) the company of men.

Describing himself as "gay, sexually adventurous, and currently (perpetually) single," Swallows began writing erotica – though he really thinks of it as porn – in 2023.

The stories included in this volume, and the details, encounters, descriptions and men, are real.

*Adventures with Men* is his first book.

Much of this bio, naturally, is fiction.

# ADVENTURES WITH MEN

## SCENES FROM A LIFE

## PAUL SWALLOWS

ERECTUS PUBLICATIONS

# ERECTUS

ISBN: 978-1-923000-79-7

BP#00132

Erectus Publications
32 Meredith Street
Sefton Park  SA  5083
Australia

Email: truthserumpress@live.com.au
Erectus webpage: truthserumpress.net/catalogue/erectus-publications/


Cover design copyright © Matt Potter
Cover image (free) copyright © calibra


Also available as an ePub eBook
ISBN: 978-1-923000-80-3
Also available as a Kindle eBook
ISBN: 978-1-923000-81-0

Erectus Publications and Truth Serum Press
are members of the
**Bequem Publishing collective**
bequempublishing.com

In memory,

to D.H.

# CONTENTS

1   BULL JUICE

6   HANGIN' OUT WITH THE LOW-HANGERS

12   BALLGAGGING AT THE SAUNA

20   FUCKED ON THE TOILET FLOOR

25   KEEPING MY DIGNITY ... ?

31   CREAMING MY WAFFLE

39   DADDY DIGS TRENCH

45   PACKAGE DELIVERED

52   A CUP OF CUM

61   THREE COINS IN MY ARSEHOLE

69   FOLDS OF FORESKIN

78   A FUCKING BLESSING

86   RIDING THE TOURIST TRAIL

93   FIRENZE FOURSOME

100   SÌ BELLO, ARRIVEDERCI

TOOLING THE TENNIS CHAMP    107

SHOWER SCENE    112

DREAM IT, THEN CREAM IT    117

I MAKE A PORNO    125

GROOMING    131

BACKSEAT BUKKAKE BLISS    137

RAMMED AT BOTH ENDS    144

THANK YOU FOR SITTING ON MY FACE    151

EVERYTHING REALLY IS A PENIS    158

CHAIN FUCK    164

THE FUCKLIST    169

TOILET TAG TEAM    177

PARTY IN THE PUB CAR PARK    186

PRIVATE PARTY, PUBLIC PARK    193

SAUNA SLING PARTY    200

SOUNDS OF PLEASURE, SOUNDS OF PAIN    204

# RANDOMS

# BULL JUICE

The hotel room door is slightly ajar but still, our knuckles rap on the wood.

The door swings open and the dom muscle bull is standing there, naked ... thick veiny cock semi-hard between his legs, low-swinging balls already churning in their sack. He's swigging a beer from what's left of a six-pack on the table. He raises his beer at us, grinning, and turning so we see his perfectly rounded arse, he waves us in.

He swigs from his beer again and we see his broad hairy chest with brown nipples the size of pennies, and wide shoulders, toned legs ... and judging by the swing of his growing cock, he's very happy to see us.

"On your knees," he says, smiling.

So we pull off our clothes – both our cocks are hard, standing to attention – and we kneel on the floor.

He saunters over and waves his growing cock in our faces. Beads of pre-cum glisten on the end of his cockhead.

"Which of you blokes wants my cum pumping inside his arse and which of you blokes wants my piss gushing down his throat?" the bull asks.

"I need your piss down my throat, sir," I say. "I drink straight from the tap."

You open your mouth to answer but the bull grabs the back of your head and thrusts his cock inside. It's a mouthful, and you gag. His balls smash against your chin as his cock thrusts deep deep deep inside your mouth. Closing your eyes, you taste sweat and pre-cum and a tantalising hint of piss.

You open your eyes and look over at me as you breathe, smelling his sweaty pubes and funky balls … he's pushing three fingers down my throat, making me suck and lick and eat them.

He pulls his fingers out of my mouth and bending over you as you continue sucking on his throbbing cock, he starts playing with your hole, his fingers wet and sloppy from my mouth. He opens your hole up and your hole accepts all three fingers. You wish he was using more fingers, all his fingers, all five of them up to the knuckle.

"Relax your hole," he says.

You do as you're told, and relax open your hole around his fingers. They're filling you up, splitting your hole wider and you wish he was using his whole fist. He pushes his fingers in deeper, rubbing your prostate. You moan, his fingers in your arse and his cock in your mouth.

I'm watching you writhe and listening to you moan as you're spit-roasted on his cock and his hand.

I am envious. Still on my knees, I look up at the muscle bull. "I need your piss now, sir," I say.

"You ready for it, fella?" he says.

"Yes, sir," I say.

"Hold on," he says. He pulls his fingers out of your arse and his cock out of your mouth. He swigs from his beer again. "Stand up."

We both stand up. He looks you in the eye, then smiling, smiling, launches a big gob of spit in your face.

You can feel it hot and sticky on your cheeks and eyes and nose and mouth. You lick your lips. You want to ask for more, but –

"Don't be greedy, mate," he says.

Then he turns to me and spits a big gob in my face. I lick my lips, it's stuck on my chin, too, so I wipe it with my fingers and lick it off each finger, savouring his sticky taste.

I want to ask him for more gob …

But our cocks are even harder now, cockheads red and wet with pre-cum.

Instead, I say, "Can I drink your piss now, sir?"

He pushes me back down to the floor. "Open your mouth."

I open my mouth, he grasps his meaty cock, throws his head back, and releases a strong hot stream of piss into my willing mouth.

I gulp it down. His piss is warm and salty but I'm so thirsty and I want every last drop of his hot steamy sulphury muscle bull piss.

You want his warm piss too so you kneel on the floor next to me and he splashes your face with flicks of his hot piss. You open your mouth, lick your lips, sampling every tasty drop.

But fuck you! I want more, I want what I deserve so I grab his cock, clamp my lips around the head and chug his hot piss down. It's streaming down my throat, filling me up.

I'm on my knees in a strange hotel room with you and a dom muscle bull who's urinating gushing streams of his hot piss down my throat. Nothing makes me feel more complete. I'd sigh, but my mouth is full.

"I want some, too," you say.

"Too bad," the bull says, pulling his cock out of my mouth. "All gone."

He smiles at you, though. "Get on the bed, arse in the air," he says.

You scramble onto the bed, arse facing him, hole open in the air, relaxed.

Just to let you know he's thinking of you, he releases a short stream of piss across your arse, then spits on your hole, and slowly … slowly … pushes his thick … veiny … meaty … sweaty cock into your open … gaping … expectant hole.

"Brace yourself, fella," he says.

His cock stretches your hole wide, wider, you can't believe it's so much thicker than his three fingers. He slides in deep, deep, soooo deep his balls slap against your perineum. Your eyes pop and you gasp.

"Stick your cock in his mouth," he says to me.

I scoot around to your face. Your mouth is open, gasping for breath and gasping in pleasure, and I push my own hard thick cock deep into your mouth. Your mouth widens and your teeth slacken and you shudder at the pleasure of two cocks pushing into either end of you.

We're rocking back and forth in rhythm, cocks thrusting into you. You're moaning, you're groaning, your tongue runs around my cock and your arsehole clamps around bull-cock, cocks pushing deeper into your guts and deeper down your gullet. Your arse has never felt so wanted and your mouth is gagging for cum.

The bull leans forward and gurgling, spits in my face again. It's warm and sticky across my nose and lips. Fuck, I want more gob, I want it smeared across my face, hot and sticky and juicy but suddenly my arse clenches. "I need to cum, sir," I say.

He thrusts deeper into your arse.

"I need to cum, sir."

He smiles at me, a sexy devil grin.

"Sir, I need to –"

"Fill 'im up," the bull says, as clasping your hips, he thrusts harder and deeper and faster.

So I clench my arse more, thrust twice more deep into your mouth … then … aaaah, release thick streams of cum far down your throat. Phft … phft … phft … phft … phft …

I smile, happy to be filling you with my hot thick creamy cum.

Phft … phft …

"Don't swallow it," the bull orders, slapping you on the arse with his hand, then "Kiss him now," he says to me.

I slowly pull my cock out of your mouth, wiping the last drops of cum across your lips. Licking your lips clean with your tongue, you look up at me as I bend down and slide my tongue inside your mouth, my sticky cum rolling around our tongues and across our teeth. We savour it, creamy and warm and hot and tasty.

Then the bull groans and throwing his head back again, pushes his cock so hard inside your guts you gulp … and balls deep, he pumps his own giant spurts of cum inside you. Phft … phft … phft … phft … phft …

You smile. You can feel each pulse in his cock against your hole, filling you up.

Phhhfffft … phft … ph-ft ………. phft …

The bull pulls his cock out, slaps his cock against your arse, and says, "On your back."

You flip over onto your back. He pushes your knees onto your chest, then looking at me, says "Now clean him up."

The bull stands back, and I scoot around to your gaping hole. His cum drips out of your arse, so I drop to my knees and sticking my fingers inside your hole, pull out gobs of his sticky hot bull cum. I lick my fingers clean, sliding his jizz around my mouth with my tongue, then plunge my tongue inside your quivering hole, licking it out, pulling your hips towards me, sucking out all his hot fuck juice, your hole wet and welcome and gaping and twitching with pleasure.

But why aren't you moaning? Glancing up, I see your head loll back as the bull kneels beside you and pushes his cock inside your mouth.

"Jerk yourself off," he orders you. With my tongue cleaning, licking, probing your wrecked hole and his hot spent sweaty cock in your mouth, it only takes you five quick strokes and your cock gushes forth with a thick stream of cum across your stomach and chest.

I can't help it.

I see that cum glistening on your body.

Now bending over you, I lick it up off your stomach and chest and then seeing your open lips, push my tongue inside your mouth, sharing its creamy taste with you.

"Gimme some," the bull says, his cock resting like a thick snake between his legs.

So standing up, I lean over and kiss him too, sharing your cum with him, sliding your cum onto his tongue, and making him taste the very last of his own steamy sulphury piss, too.

"Hang on," he says. "I'm gonna piss again."

Together, you and I scramble to our knees, mouths open, waiting, expectant, desperate for his hot piss to wet us down and slake our thirst for more bull juice.

# HANGIN' OUT WITH THE LOW-HANGERS

I'm partial to a hung tradie freeballing inside his overalls, cock ready to spring out of the fly when it's hot and moist and begging for release.

And young tradies get a lotta press. They're hot, they're hungry, they're good with their hands, they're sweaty, they're built, they're good-looking, direct, they're mobile, they're hands-on, a phone call away, they're useful, they're working, and they're every-fuckin'-where!

But what about older tradies? Tradies with a bit of experience behind (and in front of!) them, who know their way around a man's body and know all about cavities and how to fill them?

Whether they're sparkies, brickies, or chippies (and no, plumbers are not 'shitties'), tradies of all types get my cock bouncing in my shorts, and if they have some know-how and a lot of talent behind their patter (and their batter) then I'm on my knees before them.

A maintenance bloke came over earlier today.

I fucking hate cleaning gutters, and I live in a very green neighbourhood, big trees everywhere. Beautiful place to live but jeez – the leaves! And with the end of autumn coming, the gutters are chockers with the bastards. The first big winter rain we get, the rain's gonna run off the roof and not even have half-a-chance of flushing down the gutters and through the drainpipes and out into the stormwater drains.

Now I love watersports but flooding water from arsehole to breakfast time is no joke. So I find the name of a bloke who cleans gutters online – Clean Gutters 'R' You, the business is called – and he comes over within an hour. Great service … but he's here so quick, business can't be booming.

I watch as he parks his van in the driveway and jumps out. I switched the rooms in my house around so I can see the tradies and delivery guys walk up the driveway through the window near my work desk. And as he closes the van behind him, clicking the keylock and pushing it into the pocket of his shorts, I note his lean muscled calves and how the cuffs of his shorts cut tight across each toned thigh. Navy blue cap on his head and wearing a navy blue work shirt tucked into his shorts, he looks very business tradesman, but friendly, too.

I open the door to a bloke about my age, so early 50s: lean and toned, so very well put together. Dark chest hair with a sprinkling of grey poking above his work shirt, he sticks out his hand.

"Bill," he introduces himself, looking at me with the bluest of blue eyes set either side of a long, slightly pointy nose. His open clean-shaven face, tanned with sexy smile lines around his eyes, makes me hope that tan extends across his entire body. And if his long, slightly pointy nose is any indicator … ?

"I hear you need some gutters cleaned," Bill says, grinning. "Getting in before the winter deluge?"

I shake his hand, but without releasing it, clasp my other hand over it, like it's imperative we get along. And looking into his blue, blue eyes, "Yeah, g'day, mate," I say. "Glad you could come to the rescue."

Standing outside, I point to where the problem lies: the guttering along the back of the house, closest to the three massive gum trees and the screen of pines lining the back fence. "Beautiful trees," I tell him, "and they give me a shitload of privacy, but a bugger when it comes to gutter maintenance."

He looks at me with his bluest of blue eyes and says, "Looks like a simple enough job. I can start now, if you want."

Business really can't be booming.

7

"Take all the time you need, mate," I say, clasping my hands in front of me. I want to clasp my hands around his hips instead and draw him close, grind my pelvis into his, experience some honest to god sex with an equal partner, not a trade-off where I'm the older 'sir' ploughing a young guy's hole or the son fawning before a muscle bear's need to dominate like I've been doing recently. Maybe flip-flop: he fucks me / I fuck him; maybe a drink and a laugh and honest conversation. Maybe dinner too, or just a beer, which might end up pissed all over – and in – me. Yeah, I think, that would be good.

He looks at me, questioning. "You okay, mate? You seem to have drifted off there for a bit."

"Yeah, sure, all good."

"I need to change into my other work gear," he says, "then I'll bring my ladder around and start."


Bill has changed into his other work gear: a cloth cap and long-sleeved navy blue shirt for the sun, and different shorts. Shorter shorts, floppier and with a wider leg. Much shorter shorts, with legs wide enough to slip my hand up and play with his cock and balls.

I watch his hands, covered in big thick work gloves, pull out bark and gum leaves and pine needles and shit from the gutter and in big sweeping arcs throw it on the paving below. He says he'll clean it up later. That's all part of his service.

I watch from inside the house. Sitting in a chair in the window, pretending to read a book, sneaking peeks at his hairy calves on the ladder leading up to his hairy thighs and his loose-legged short shorts … and heaven. Fuck, my cock is so hard I can't sit comfortably in the chair. I pull the chair closer to the window and place the book across my growing bulge. And stare at his package as it shifts and moves and twitches with each drag and pull and throw and sweeping arc.

He leans back away from the ladder a little and pulls his shorts up at the waist. And that's when I see it. Just a peek, a sneaky glimpse, a bobble, a wobble, with a light dusting of hair … a ball, one of his balls, a flash of testicle poking through the leg of his shorts.

The back door closes behind me – I want to let it slam shut but I don't want to scare his ball back inside his shorts – and I step under the ladder. And under him. And look up.

He leans away from the ladder again and looking down, catches my eye.

"Sorry, buddy," he says, and grinning, paws at the leg of his shorts with a dirty work glove. "They have a life of their own."

And somehow, by trying to adjust his shorts with an incompetent work glove, the other ball peeks out, too. It's fucking hot – they're a little hairy – not too much, just enough to grip onto with your teeth when you're sucking them to give that split-second pinch of pain.

"Don't apologise, mate," I say, reaching up as if to touch them, but missing, on purpose, for the moment. "Looks like you got a nice set on you, a handsome set of nuts to make you proud."

Bill grins and pulls his short shorts up even higher. He doesn't have just a nice set of nuts between his legs – he has a magnificent set of nuts between his legs, conkers swinging free in mid-air, massive tan knackers, like ripe fruit waiting to be picked and fondled and licked and sucked and manhandled and milked of all their juice.

I shake my head in awe. "Fuck, you got … words can't describe them, mate – amazing AMAZING low-hangers. I am almost – ALMOST – lost for words." I reach up, just as he steps down a rung. His nuts fall into my hands, soft and silky and rolling in their sack. And I see a wet patch at the front of his shorts.

"Man, that feels good," he says, still standing on the ladder. "It's been too long since a fit fella touched 'em up."

I'm balancing them in my hand, gently weighing them. I pull his low-hangers down, stretch the skin, ring my fingers around the sack and really yank them down. Bill groans, rocking on the ladder with pleasure. "Fuck!" he whispers. "Hang on."

I release my grip as he pulls his shorts down, steps out of them while still holding on to the ladder, kicks them off. I reach for his shorts as they fall, hoping to suck up that patch of pre-cum, but they land on the ground on top of fetid bark and leaves and needles and shit.

"You always freeball on the job?" I ask as he steps down another rung. Now it's easy – grabbing his balls again and pulling, he gasps. My tongue darts at his glistening knob. I breathe in and sniff his long, veiny cock, smell his funky tradie sweat along the shaft, caress his churning balls. Still clasping them in my hand, I nip around to the other side of the ladder and am faced with his beautiful arse. It's lightly hairy, man-funky, taut and round, and ripe for the eating.

I look up and he nods in agreement, in enjoyment, holding on to the ladder as he bends his knees and lowers his arse on to my face, his hole over my mouth. I stick my tongue inside his crack, licking, biting, searching for entry. His hips twitch and his hole relaxes. I spit on his hole and dig up and dig in, hard and probing further, fucking his hole with my tongue. I want to get deep inside him, open him up and really taste all he has to offer. You might find me on all fours in the toilets drinking a hot muscle bull's piss or fucking a hot young dude on his back in my bed but when I get my tongue inside a hot hole, I want to reach into his very soul.

He pushes his arse back against my face and breathes out in a rush.

I release my grip on his balls, grab his hips and with a GRRUUUNT, pull his arse hard down onto me.

His back arches and his hole smashes onto my lips.

Feasting on his fuckhole, scraping it with my teeth, incisors gnashing on his sphincter, digging deep inside, I want all of him.

One hand on the ladder, he grabs his cock and starts pulling, jerking his meat so his balls bounce back and forth as I slather down his arse juice.

"Fuck," he whispers. Then, "Oh mate," he moans.

I reach up so my nose is in his hole too, ramming against him. I want him on a fucking plate, want to reach up through his arsehole to his stomach and his heart and his mouth and his brain.

It's so fucking primal!

His body shudders as I grip his balls and tug harder.

"Fuck!!" he says, jerking his cock at incredible speed. And reeling with the pressure I'm forcing upwards and the shock in his balls and the fury in his yanking, he totters on the ladder.

I quickly grab the ladder with both hands.

He grabs the gutter above.

The ladder teeters to a stop.

"Whoa," I say, glad to have stopped our highwire act from crashing.

"Fuck, that's intense," he says, lifting his arse an inch off my face. "You nearly made me cum."

My face is wet with his arse juice and my spit. With his knees still bent, his cock level with my lips, I nip around and clamp my mouth around his cockhead. Pulling his balls to anchor him, tongue caressing his cockhead, hand working his shaft back-forth-back-forth-back-forth-back-forth-back-forth-back-forth-back-forth, I suck deep and strong.

"Oh," he gasps, hands clasping the top of my head, "fuck mate, I don't wanna cum ... ooh ..." but it's too late. And I earn my reward, as he shoots giant streams of sweet, sweet mancum in my mouth. I relax my lips around his cockhead as I chug down every sticky, thick creamy drop of fuckjuice, tasting it on my tongue, sliding it down my throat, then throwing my head back as it drains down my gullet.

I wipe my mouth with the back of my hand, like I've finally drunk my fill.

His knees shake as he steps down the ladder. "I gotta get to another job," he says, but then he stops and looks me in the eye. "Fuck mate, that's the best rim job I've ever had. Can I buy you a beer?"

I was right – business isn't booming ... 'cos he stays all afternoon.

At the end of the day, the bad thing is, the gutter's still chockers with bark and leaves and needles and shit.

But the good thing is, he's coming back tomorrow for a rematch. And he's bringing a sturdier ladder.

# BALLGAGGING
# AT THE SAUNA

10 cocks.

  5 loads.

  2 – 3 – 4 hours in the sling.

  'Dom Night' at the sauna.

But it's the wrong fucking Thursday night! It's not Dom Night at the sauna, it's 'Nerd Night' instead.

Nerd Night!? Who came up with that fucking idea?

Soaping my legs in the communal shower, playing with my cock, cupping my balls, warm water running over my arse and down my crack, I console myself with wisdom from the film 'Revenge of the Nerds': that nerds spend so much time thinking about sex (and not getting any) that when they do get it, they're fucking amazing at it.

My only two accessories are poppers and a ballgag. Poppers bottle sits on the ledge nearby, and the ballgag I'm wearing as I shower. It buckles up behind my ears, and is made of black leather with a silver buckle, but the ball is red rubber on a spindle. So it moves with my tongue.

But I'm earning a lot of pervy looks as I shower, ballgag in place. One bloke, bad black toupée clamped on his freckly head, stands at the end of the showers and openly stares.

I turn the shower off, towel myself dry, grab my poppers, check ballgag is firmly in place (and breathe through my nose) and head for the steam room.

I saunter around the plinth in the middle of the steam room – an older bloke lies stomach down, arse up – and I catch the eye of as many men as possible as I walk past. Two young Asian muscle studs.

A couple in their 40s – though hard to tell through all the steam! But I'm hard to miss, with the red rubber ball gagging me, even in the rush of fog.

It's not easy to breathe in the steam room wearing a ballgag … so the door soon wheezes shut behind me and I walk past the plunge pool. No one's in the plunge pool – the only men who ever swim or dive or jump or fall into the plunge pool are usually lost for something better to do – and open the door to the sauna.

I can only stand about 30 seconds in the sauna, it's too hot! Though I was once fucked by a toned trombonist for about ten minutes from behind while I stood up, arms stretched out against the wood-panelled wall.

I saunter through the outer room, then open the creaky wooden door and step into the hotter, inner room. Men with draped towels sit on the wooden benches – a few muscled, hairy and shaved dom-types; a few hairless and very hairy nerd-types; and a few other-types – but they all watch me as I pass. Of course, they do, I'm wearing a fucking red ballgag!

But it does make me bolder. I look directly at men's cocks, eyeing them off, rubbing my hard-on through the towel, looking directly in their eyes, longer than usual, inviting them – willing them – to fuck me. Ballgag and all.

Perhaps they don't expect a fit, toned bloke in his early 50s to be wearing a red rubber ballgag.

As I walk out of the sauna, the two Asian muscle studs pass me on their way in. One has a South Korean flag tattooed on his bicep, the other some kind of dragon. Dunno about the dragon as it blurs past, but I know the flag's the South Korean flag. I know my flags. It's a thing I've always been interested in. I watch them disappear. One of them catches my eye as the sauna door shuts behind them.

I walk past the spa – the eyes of the men bubbling in the spa follow me as I saunter past – then I climb the stairs to the next floor. Walking past the cubicles on either side – some with doors closed, some doors opened, some unoccupied – I stop at the bend in the passageway. This is where I stood one lunchtime, while a younger dom lightly punched my pecs. Then spat in my face. I was outraged, heart and head hot for revenge, ready to draw back and slug him in the face … but I also felt my cock stiffen under my towel, and as I licked his gob off my face, I wanted him to do it again.

As I stand at the half-open door to the sling room, moans sound from a nearby cubicle. Hope they don't shoot their loads so they're too spent to join me later. I'm in the mood to take on all cummers.

I slide the door to the sling room across. Thankfully, the sling is empty. (It's that quiet time between the after-work crowd and the after-dinner crowd.) I step inside, hang my towel on a hook in the dim light, push my arse up to the edge of the sling, grab the chains either side of me, and lean back. It's not an easy move. You see porn stars do it and you wonder how! Just slide back onto the sling? It takes some nudging of my hips and rocking of my shoulders to get into the right position, and when I'm lying back, waiting for cock #1 (whoever, whenever, however that will be), I link my legs around the chains, exposing my hole. I breathe out, sink into the rubber of the sling, and clutching the poppers bottle on my stomach, wait.

The door slides shut and I glimpse a hand latching it closed. (Of course, some bloke was waiting in the corner, in the shadows, breath unnoticeable!) He stands in the dim light between my open legs. He's pale and tall (good, I like tall), with a thick mat of dark, dark hair on his chest and stomach (good, I like hairy), and a slight paunch under nicely rounded pecs and wide shoulders (more to grab onto as he fucks me) atop a rangy frame. He leans over me, so I feel his bush and growing cock against mine.

(The bush is a sign he's not so interested in the way he looks. Otherwise, he'd be manscaping.)

He bites my left nipple, licks it, bites it, licks it, then onto my right nipple – bites it, licks it, bites it, licks it. I shudder and shiver and push my pelvis against his body, grinding it up and in.

He pulls away and nudges his cock under my churning balls, his knob rubbing my twitching pucker. My hole opens wide to welcome cock, needing to be fucked, fucked deep, fucked deep and long, fucked deep and long and hard and sweaty. Fucked so it's taken and fucked so it's owned.

But don't mistake me for a sub. This is not submission. This is collusion.

I wish he'd slide the door open – I like an audience.

It's half-dark, and I've got the red rubber ballgag in my mouth so even if I talk, my words are garbled. But our bodies do the talking. He grips the chains on either side and pushes his lubed-up cock past my pucker and keeps on going, slowly, expertly, feeling every millimetre of my fucktube as it closes around his meat. Deep. I can take a long cock but fuck! his is loooong. Long and lean, like his body. And he's smiling, enjoying my arse already, snug around his meat. He nods as he slides in and out of my hole. My so-hard cock bounces against my stomach. Touch it and it'll likely explode.

I wish we were being watched, feet creaking on the floorboards as guys saunter in, stand around, stroke their meat, suck each other off, pinch and turn and twist and grind my nipples, as this tall rangy guy ploughs my fuckhole. And would he step aside and allow other men to take turns on my hole? Isn't that why I'm in the sling?!

But the door is still latched shut.

"Nice?" he asks.

I nod. Yes sir, I think. And clamp my ring around his fuckstick.

His mouth opens with pleasure, and he giggles. He looks at me but even in the semi-dark his eyes look a little unfocussed. He closes them, and starts up an earnest rhythm, cock and hole, hole and cock.

I breathe in and breathe out. He's working my hole, in out, in out. Not touching my cock. Yes sir, I'm thinking, cock bouncing on its own. Yes sir, fuck me, yes sir, in out, yes sir, yes sir, yes sir, fuck me, yes sir, yes sir, fuck me, fuck me, yes sir, in out, yeeeessssirrrrr.

It's deeper, lodged deeper in my manhole, drilling deep, him grunting, me gasping through the red rubber ballgag. Fuck – fuck – fuck … he's holding it there, and I gasp again, strangled through the red rubber ball.

Hold it.

Clamp my ring around it.

Deep ...

A knock on the door. Three knocks.

Tall Guy pulls out of my hole, unlatches the door, and another lanky dude enters. Lanky Dude latches the door behind him, drops his towel on the floor, hands something to Tall Guy, and Tall Guy slips on a pair of glasses.

Question answered. I'm definitely not being fucked by a dom.

Tall Guy steps back and Lanky Dude assumes centre stage, hard cock poised against my pucker. He's also wearing glasses – I see reflections on the lenses in the dim light – and is a little shorter than Tall Guy but just as pale, and possibly thinner, with a light covering of (ginger?) hair on his chest.

Lanky Dude grabs my hips and – there's enough lube in my hole already – pushes his cock inside me. He's thicker than his mate, and not so long, but it's touching the sides and if he loads my hole and Tall Guy jumps in afterwards and loads my hole, that's 2 cocks and 2 loads down, with only 8 cocks and 3 loads to go.

Why am I'm obsessing about numbers?

Tall Guy stands by my face, stroking his meat. I can smell my arse juice on his cock and pubes, and curse the ballgag, as I'd be chowing down on that cock now if I wasn't half-choking on a red rubber ball. But Lanky Dude's cock is hitting the spot, so I settle in as he rides me, fucks me, yes sir, I'm thinking. Yes sir, indeed.

As Lanky Dude fucks, I look up at Tall Guy, eyes wide, ballgag lodged in my mouth. Tall Guy jerks his cock, pulling the skin back, rubbing it forward, and smiles at me, so I look at him earnestly, eyes pleading for connection. He rubs his cockhead on my face, smears his pre-cum on my cheekbone, touches my face with his hand, sticky with pre-cum and lube and my arse. I start tonguing the red rubber ball, rolling it on the spindle in my mouth. Tall Guy smiles again, and dips his cockhead onto it, wipes his pre-cum across it, which I lick off as the ball rolls with my tongue.

I unscrew the lid on the poppers, and as Lanky Dude pulls his cock out of my hole then pushes it through my pucker, take a big huff. Out of my hole, then slams it back in. Another big huff. Out of my hole. Slams it back in.

My head fills with that sudden warm hot fuzz, and I spread my legs wider hoping for more cock, more cum, harder deeper jackhammering. I love poppers. I want the hot fuzz to last forever.

Lanky Dude senses my need and ups his game, slamming hips and pelvis and cock into me. SLAM and SLAM and SLAM and SLAM. I moan through the ballgag and want more poppers, but the SLAM and SLAM and SLAM and opening a small bottle of chemicals and SLAM and SLAM and SLAM is not gonna work. There's a gleam in Tall Guy's eyes too, behind his glasses, and he's working his cock harder too, directing it at my face. His piss slit is slick with pre-cum and fuck fuck fuck this ballgag! I want that cum shooting into my mouth and sliding down my throat. I look into Tall Guy's eyes – LOOK AT ME, FUCKER! – and he looks at me and smiles and points his cockhead directly at the ballgag and I start rolling the red rubber ball with my tongue. Lanky Dude SLAMS my arse – SLAM and SLAM and SLAM and SLAM – and Tall Guy throws his head back and jerks his meat and groans and pulls HARD on his cock and Lanky Dude grabs my hips and STOPS just in time as Tall Guy shoots his fuckin' thick creamy load on the ballgag and my lips and chin and I'm working my tongue furiously to spin the ballgag. I taste his load in my mouth and on my tongue and want it down my throat and sliding into my gullet. It's NOT ENOUGH, it's just a taste and I want more! So I scrape the cum on my lips and chin with my fingers onto the ball and spin it some more, savouring his white-hot jizz, and look up at Tall Guy, wishing he had more cum to share, eyes pleading for one more drop of hot manjuice.

Tall Guy smears the last drops of cum on my chin. Taking off his glasses, he wipes his eyes and nose with the back of his hand, his softening cock resting near my jaw.

I unscrew the lid of the poppers and take a big huff, then another then another, swapping nostrils, then another, then another and another, deeeeep hufffssss.

Lanky Dude, taking the cue, starts on my fuckhole again, pushing in and pulling out. I hand the poppers to Tall Guy just as Lanky Dude gains momentum, cock punching in deep, deep, deeper. I want his cum deep in my thirsty hole. Then it's SLAM and SLAM and SLAM and SLAM and SLAM and SLAM again as I grip the chains and tilt my pelvis up so his cock punches deeper again. I gasp at his might, his glasses slipping down his nose as sweat drips off his forehead and nose and chin. This fucking nerd owns me!

Tall Guy leans over and takes Lanky Dude's glasses off his nose. Lanky Dude leans over me and grabs my shoulders, pushes my body onto his grinding cock. I'm almost doubled up as his cock punches into me. SLAM – SLAM – SLAM – SLAM. I cry out behind the red rubber ballgag.

Lanky Dude lets out a long, low growling moan, and pulling into me, I tighten my ring around his fuckpole as he shoots his fucking hot cumload into my arse, spurt after roping spurt after spurt after spurt after spurt after spurt – spurt – spurt … spurt … …

I'm still half-hunched as he pulls out, and leaning over me, he kisses the red rubber ball in my mouth and laughs. I let out a kind of laugh, too. Good sex always makes me laugh. It's part of the release.

Lanky Dude steps around to my face and rubs his cummy, sweaty cock against my other cheekbone. It smells of arsejuice and cock.

The two men sigh with exhaustion and pick up their towels off the floor. I grab the chains and pull myself up to sit on the edge of the sling. Lanky Dude nods and smiles, and Tall Guy pats my shoulder in thanks, then puts the poppers on a small shelf by the dimmer switch. The door unlatches, slides half-open, and the two men step out and are gone.

That was perfect. The perfect cock tag team.

But I'm fucked. My hole is fucking sore and needs a break. I should take the ballgag off for a while. Check my jaw is working again. Pick up my poppers and head for the showers.

And then I hear the door slide open a little further, and two men step inside. Latching the door closed, I spy a tattoo of a South Korean flag on one bicep, and a definite dragon on another.

I smile (as much as I can with the ballgag still in place), and leaning back onto the sling, I open my legs and slip my feet around the chains snaking above me. Spying the bottle of poppers on the shelf, Dragon Man grabs them, then steps behind me, and grabbing my arms, pins them behind my head. Just as Flag Man kneels between my legs, opens my gaping manhole with his fingers, and starts lapping at it, licking it, sucking it and eating it, with his quick, silky, probing tongue.

Dragon Man leans forward and tweaks my nips. I groan, so he pinches them harder, pushes them in, grinds them under his fingers. Then he uncaps the bottle and waves the poppers under my nose and I huff. A big huff. Another big huff. Another big, loooong huffff. And my head is in that rushed, warm, fuzzy place again.

Nerds so far?

Not sure.

Cocks so far?

Four probably.

Loads so far?

Two … and counting.

# FUCKED ON THE
# TOILET FLOOR

I love the Indian men at the local shopping centre. Tight shorts and torso-hugging polo shirts, they collect trolleys in the car parks and push them back to the trolley corrals or inside the supermarkets. Calves stretching, thighs straining, wide backs expanding, giving admirers (and me) a free show.

We stand at a pedestrian crossing waiting to cross the busy road between two busy shopping centres. Prakash – so his badge says – is about 30, wearing tight shorts and a polo shirt, but the sleeves are long and loose, falling over his biceps as he pushes them back up his arm. I'm sure he's doing this for me. I WANT to help him, reach across and roll his sleeves up so they stay tight around his tawny, toned, gym-worked biceps. But 11.45am on a busy Friday, on the busiest road stretching north of the city, is probably not the best time.

He catches my eye for a second, smiles. He is ball-grindingly handsome: deep brown eyes, glossy skin, and a moustache waxed at the tips, just slightly at each end, like a suave '30s film star. It's hard not to stare at him, but I keep catching looks as we wait for the lights to change. Others wait at the kerb too, vague background figures. Prakash looks ahead, stealing sideways looks at me when he thinks I'm not – or I am – looking.

My cock stirs in my jocks.

Lights change red. Brakes squeal. Engines idle. Green man flashes us the go-ahead.

I step aside as Prakash congas the shopping trolleys down the slight ramp and across the road. He's carrying a backpack on his back but it's his arse I'm watching, in his navy shorts, rubbing against the cotton.

My cock rubs against the cotton of my jocks as I walk directly behind him, eyes glued to his glutes. I imagine dropping to my knees and pulling his cheeks apart, dipping my tongue inside his crack, probing his hole, pushing his butt open, spreading the love.

As the line of trolleys catches in the lip of the opposite ramp, I step closer behind him and catch a whiff of his cologne. He bends forward to put more muscle into it, pushing with his arms and shoulders and back. I pass on his right, brush past his arse and shoulder, barely touching but touching still.

As I step off the kerb, I look behind me and catch him looking at me again, give a split-second smile, hoping he's noting my firm arse in my shorts, my wide shoulders in my t-shirt. Spying a bench nearby, I sit down. Digging into my pocket, I pull out a shopping list. 'Carrots for soup', it says.

Prakash meanders the trolley line past me on the bench, looks at me again, just slightly – slightly – but a smile plays on his lips. I watch his head, his shoulders, his arms, his arse, his legs – and his backpack – as they slowly file into the shopping centre. Automatic doors glide shut behind them.


I bought the carrots. A big bag.

But I hang around. Sit on a bench inside the shopping centre. Watch people mill past in the bright neon. Watch Prakash as he collects more trolleys, lines them up, pushes them together. Watch as he files them into the supermarket.

He's conscious of his moustache – he twirls the ends of it, like a villain with an evil laugh – but he's so fucking sexy with it. And his arse is working overtime in his shorts, bending and stretching, and those meaty calves – fuck! I want them wrapped around me!

I'm touching up the carrots, feeling them, thick and hard, through the plastic. My hand runs along the shaft, pumping a large carrot like it's a throbbing cock. My own cock is stiff and aching for release in my jocks.

My jaw tightens as I see Prakash, backpack still across his shoulders, talk to some supermarket staffer. Looks like he's knocking off for lunch.

I stand up from the bench, holding the carrots in front of me, pressing them against my hard-on.

Prakash looks over at me, almost nods his head. Almost.

I step away from the bench, amble off to the right, keeping almost eye contact. Prakash steps out of the supermarket, walks off to his left.

Ambling through the centre, I turn right down a passageway and head past the 'Toilets' sign. Shoes scuff on floor tiles behind me. Turning right again, the wheelchair sign sticks out from the wall above on the left. Ten more paces and I slide the door open to the accessible toilet, step inside. The door slides closed but I leave it open, just a crack.

Footsteps on the tiles, tawny fingers slide the door open. Holding my breath, hot Indian guy slips through the door, slides it closed slowly behind him, deftly locks the door, '30s Hollywood moustache smiles at me … FUCK! he's standing before me, slipping the backpack off his shoulders and stashing it in the corner.

Shorts unbutton and slip down his sculpted legs to the floor. He's wearing big workboots and thick white socks, and I hope he keeps them on. And he does! stepping out of his shorts, he rips off the polo shirt with ease and tosses it over the backpack, name badge clattering against the wall. He stands wearing a jockstrap, a big wet patch at the front. Broad chest, hair in all the right places, sly smile, trim gym-fit waist, beefy thighs – man, he's done this before!

And those nipples! Brown and hard and ripe for licking and tasting and biting … but what the fuck do I do with this big bag of carrots?!

Prakash takes the carrots from my hands and drops them beside his backpack. I don't want to waste time so I sink to my knees. He pulls his cock out from his jock. It's hard – fucking hard – and meaty and uncut and funky and veiny and leaking and I grab his balls with my hands and pulling close, slide my lips around the head and slip my mouth over the shaft, down, deep down so his pubes brush my nose, all the way in, an impressive feat, an amazing mouthful.

He pushes his pelvis against me, his cock wedged down my throat. Hands clasping my head, he draws into me. I gag, then he slowly slides his meat out then slowly slides it back in, savouring every millimetre of meat and man and musk and mouth.

Prakash pulls out past my lips and turning round, opens his backpack and pulls out a thick blanket, which he unfolds and hard cock bouncing over his jock, spreads across the floor.

Man, he's done this before!

But I want his cock in my mouth still, tasting its juices, licking his pre-cum, breathing his jockfunk. He pushes me on the shoulders, so I lean back and he pushes me further, 'til I sit on my arse and lie back on the blanket. He squats down and pulls my shorts down over my shoes, then whips my jocks off, too. Devilish moustache twinkling above his full lips, he's a man possessed but he knows what he's doing. Head lolling, looking up at the ceiling, I close my eyes and hear the rustle of plastic and the squelch of lube. I breathe out, pull my knees up onto my chest, relax, open my hole.

Prakash touches my hole with a wet finger. I want to connect with him, watch his face as he slides his cock into me but the fluoro lights shining down from the ceiling are bright. I close them. "Fuck me," I whisper.

My hole twitches as something hard slowly slides inside. I reach down around my arse and feel for his cock as it delves deeper into my hole. But it's not a big thick cock my fingers touch. I open my eyes but the fluoros are blinding. Looking on the floor, I spy the plastic bag ripped open, carrots spilling on the floor.

The skin I caress is knobbly under my fingertips. And then I realise – he's fucking me with a big thick carrot!

Man, he really HAS done this before!

I mean, this is not the first time I've been fucked in a toilet.

Nor the first time I've been fucked on a toilet floor.

But it IS the first time I've been fucked on a toilet floor with a vegetable.

I chuckle, thinking about precautions I take to protect myself.

I love PrEP. PrEP means I'm ever ready to fuck. PrEP has changed my life.

Though I don't need to be on PrEP to be fucked by a carrot.

Prakash grins as he kneels between my legs, pushes the carrot deep inside my hole. My hips spread so he pushes in deeper, my ring twitching, my stomach spasming with each gritty thrust and twist of his wrist. My hole is hungry. I really want his cock deep inside me but animal? vegetable? mineral? who cares?! He smiles as my cock throbs against my stomach, my fuckhole full and tight and grasping. I'm leaning back on my elbows, feet in the air and legs spread wide so I can't jerk my straining cock, but it's my hole that's feeling all the rough, rapid, in-out in-out in-out pleasure.

I look at his cockhead slick with pre-cum, throbbing between his knees. Then he groans, releases his grip on the carrot. Kneeling up, he pulls on his cock, taut foreskin straining against the shaft. He grunts. Shoots ropes of cum in a creamy arc across the floor tiles: spurt after spurt after thick sticky dripping gasping spurt.

He shudders, naked arse sinking back on the heels of his workboots, hand and cock hanging loose. His moustache tips droop a little under his devilish smile. But I want his cum in my mouth, on my tongue, down my gullet. So as he shakes the last cum drop on the floor, I roll over onto my knees. Reaching behind, I shove the carrot so deep inside me my eager pucker swallows it whole. And leaning forward, my tongue licks every pool, every streak, every splatter, every sprog drop off the floor.

I flick his cum around my mouth. As Prakash watches wide-eyed, I tilt my head back. Each gritty gob slides down, down into my gullet. I breathe out after my epic swallow. And smile.

Prakash points at a cum-blob I've missed, glossy in the light. But before I lunge to suck it off the floor, he swipes it up with both index fingers, rubs it against his thumbs, and just slightly twists both tips of his moustache, perking them up.

# KEEPING MY DIGNITY ... ?

Things I really love:
• books
• sex
• Avenue 2Q Books and Novelties.

Avenue 2Q Books and Novelties actually sells books, with real men in the shop opening books but only looking at the pictures. Real men reading back covers like they're devouring Nobel Prize-winning literature (but not really). Real men adjusting their bulges hoping some real man's watching.

And it has booths out the back.

The crowd varies depending upon the time of day. Visit mid-afternoon and the lunchtime married cocksuckers have returned to their office jobs, though serious cruisers are still hanging around.

I'm a big reader but if I'm at Avenue 2Q, I'm not there for the wordcount!

2.50pm. Hot muscle bear, heavy moustache, blue t-shirt with a giant red and yellow 'S' across his pecs, snackable cut lunch in his tight shorts.

Glances exchanged as we stand in 'Sexual Health'. He turns another page of 'The Zen of Men'. Turns away.

False start.

3.00pm. Tall, beefy but toned, greying handlebar moustache, short grey goatee, shaved head, steely blue eyes that look straight at you. I'm standing beside 'M2M Fiction – Authors L to P' while he's standing in the next aisle, on the other side of the metre-or-so high bookshelf.

Sounds, looks, smells ex-military.

Black leather jacket, and a dark blue t-shirt.

Fucking fucking commanding and fucking fucking hot.

I saunter along the aisle, round the shelves at the end.

I'm now in 'M2M Fiction – Authors C to G' and smell leather and cigar smoke. I see leather jacket a little zipped up, more blue t-shirt, and faded jeans, tight where they need to be and looser where the action is.

He replaces a book on the shelf and piercing eyes look directly at me. I pick the same book off the shelf, flip it to look at the front cover, then the back cover, look at the front again. 'Darkroom' by Nick Christie. I weigh it in my hand, like it's a big piece of meat, like I'm cupping a massive pair of balls, like I can't believe it's this heavy and I'm still able to hold it.

I look from the book to the bulge in his jeans – back to the book then up to his face. Then back to his bulge. He's playing pocket billiards, one hand flicking his hardening cock in his jeans. His steely blue gaze dares me to look away. Then he peers down at his shiny black boots.

"They need cleaning," he says.

I look down at his boots, too. "What made them so dirty?" I ask. (They don't look dirty, though.)

"Bull piss and dom cum," he says.

He must have read my wishlist.

As I stick 'Darkroom' back on the shelf he grabs my shoulders and pushes me to my knees. So I sink down to my elbows and arse sticking out one end and tongue sticking out the other, start licking his boots.

Yeah, they taste of piss and cum. And shiny leather and boot polish.

"Mmmmm – mmm," I moan. But ...

What do I do now? I'm licking his boots – the right one, then the left, then the right again, tonguing the leather, bobbing and sniffing – but I really want the dom piss and the bull cum – no, the bull piss and the dom cum! – straight from the source, pumping down my throat. Not a secondhand serving on shiny leather.

And it's kinda fun to fuck with stereotypes, too, isn't it?

So I look up at the beefy man mountain from my spot on the floor. "This is not doing much for me, mate." I stand up, stare him in his steely blue eyes. "I'm not really feeling the sub vibe today," I add. "Or the boot fetish vibe. Or the kneeling in the 'M2M Fiction' vibe." I turn and head for the booths at the back of the shop.

I look over my shoulder, see if he's following me. He's still playing pocket billiards, standing in 'C to G'. He looks through me with a bored expression, looks away. Maybe he sneers. Maybe he has a cold and needs a good sniff.

Ah, the booths. Well, a booth is a booth is a booth. 4 walls with a door and a chair. Walk in, leave the door ajar. Wait for any man of interest to sneak in and close the door behind him, then pull out his growing cock. One of us gets sucked.

And ten seconds after I leave the door ajar, steely blue eyes follows me in, closes the door behind him.

He's packing a pretty impressive bulge in the half-light of the booth, so I give him the benefit of the doubt and sink to my knees.

He wastes no time: unzips his leather jacket, undoes his jeans. He's going commando so as he pulls down his fly, his cock jumps out at me, big-headed and meaty, drops of pre-cum on his piss-slit.

Then he reaches in under his cock and lifts his balls out and – fuck me! – they are a majorly impressive sight. Three thick metal cockrings weigh them down – three! An unholy trinity! – all the same size and thickness, locked tight with an allen key, dominant and powerful and hard. And still his glorious boys swing underneath, two globes of prime beef rolling in a sack made for sucking. If he wears these three cockrings permanently then I'm impressed with his boys' stamina. Whack them about a bit and the shock'll probably register on the Richter scale.

He grabs the back of my head and pushes his throbbing cock past my lips, over my tongue and down my throat, jamming it in, so his cockrings thwack against my chin. I reach around and grab his arse, sinking my fingers into each cheek, pulling him into my face. He facefucks me, grabs my ears and drives his cock hard over my jaw and teeth and into the back of my neck, slamming his meat so far into me he's declaring sovereignty and staking his fuckpole like a land claim on my chest and my heart and my guts.

He grunts, then pulls out and slams his cock down my neck again, pulls it out and shoves it in so far and so fast my head would spin if his meaty paws weren't gripping my ears like a vice.

Pull out – slam! – pull out – slam! – pull out – slam!

I gag each time he piledrives his nasty meat into me, then recover for a second while he pulls out then it's gag-time again, cockhead filling my throat and my head so I can't breathe.

His leather jacket slaps the sides of my face with each pull backward, and in between each choke I'm lost in the pain of his grip on my ears and the expectation of more choking and gagging and the total surrender to his piledriving cock down my gullet.

Pull out – slam! – pull out – slam! – pull out – slam! – pull out – slam!

The cockrings are whacking against my chin. My clipped beard will cover any bruising the cockrings cause, but I still want to be able to eat solids. So I grab his balls and pull them away from my face. He groans, liking the extra tension of my pulling, pushes his cock down my throat again.

Now my hand hits my chin instead, so the ball-pull has given me some control.

But the angle of his cock as he pushes back into my mouth is skewed. He releases his grip on my ears, retrieves his cock from my mouth with his paw.

I release my hold on his swingers. They sway between his meaty thighs.

He looks at me with dull eyes and says, "You're a bad cocksucker, son."

Oh.

Now, I could be insulted. My throat has taken a beating and he's almost ripped my ears off. He's pounded the fuck out of my face and I'm sure he's enjoyed it.

So I should climb up off my knees. I should walk out of the shop. I should keep my dignity.

But I'm a cumslut. I'm still on my knees. And I want my creamy reward.

I'm about to say, "So cum on my face, you nasty fucker!" but he shoves his thumb in my mouth and, fingers clamping under my chin, yanks my head closer. Pre-cum and sweat fill my nostrils as he rubs his cock against my nose, my cheekbones, my eyelids, jerking, grunting, furiously stroking his cock up and down, his bull balls banging against the hand wedging my jaw open.

My eyes flick up to see handlebar moustache, short grey goatee, shaved head and steely blue eyes sneering at me … leering, scorning, jeering. Mocking me, taunting me, his lips curling with derision and disgust.

Sweat beads off his forehead and splashes into my eye, so I squeeze my eyelid shut … and then he groans, grinds his cock and breathes out … and shoots … nuts in my face, sprogs across my upper lip … nuts ropes of thick tasty cum across my moustache and the tip of my nose.

I flare my nostrils. Huff deep. Sniff long and hard. Snort his hot cum up my nose. And he keeps nutting, gripping my jaw open as he spasms … and his cock shoots … shoots more cum … I sniff again and huff more hot white cum up my nose but it's just inside my nostril, a snotty bubble of cum as I breathe out.

He loosens his grip on my jaw then pushes my head away. Grabbing the back of my head again, he wipes his cummy cockhead on my bottom lip.

I lick his cum off with my tongue.

"Good lad," he says, and chucking me under the chin, looks deep into my eyes. "Now walk out of here with my cum on your fuckin' face."

So I climb up off my knees.

And as I walk through the shop, passing the hot muscle bear with the heavy moustache, blue t-shirt with a giant red and yellow 'S' across his pecs and the snackable cut lunch in his shorts, he looks up from reading 'Zen with Men'. I smile at him, and wave, my face glowing wet with sticky bull cum.

And taking a rolling sniff and licking more sprog off my moustache with my very athletic tongue, I couldn't give a fuck about keeping my dignity.

# CREAMING MY WAFFLE

Brussels is known for chocolate, beer, moules, and waffles. I love beer, am partial to chocolate, and have eaten moules every evening since I arrived three days ago.

But waffles? The last thing I want to eat in this sticky July heat is flour-sugar-eggs-milk-butter-baking powder and whatever goes on top.

I also love men and today, all day, I was fucking horny.

At the Atomium, I was in full-on cruise mode, but it's hard to get men's attention on escalators and stairs amid multiple flights of light shows and hypnotic music.

The Musée Magritte seemed an obvious place to cruise, but the strictly get in-move along-look hypnotised by art-get out crowd didn't allow for any lingering eye contact.

And the Manneken-Pis was very crowded, and not much of a show.

I had a slow lunch at 1.30 (moules!) then walked back to my rental and jerked off. Getting serious about finding a fuck, I douched, pulled on a jockstrap, short shorts and t-shirt, and set out again. Now it's approaching 7.00 and I'm cruising again, backpack slung across my shoulders. It's summer in Europe, so there are hot men everywhere!

Plus, I'm hungry.

Strolling along a side street, I spy a waffle shop. Or smell it first, then see small tables and chairs stacked just inside the door. Behind the counter stands a man: dark and tall and thin, mid-30s and serious-looking, chiselled face with a close-cropped beard. He looks up just as I step into the shop. My cock stirs in my shorts.

"Bonjour, are you closing?" I ask.

I don't speak French but find it best to greet someone in French and then launch into English. Thus I've made the slightest effort to be international.

"Oui, we close at …"

I look at the sign on the door: the shop is open from 9.00 to 19.00 every day.

"At 7.00," he says.

"Oh." I smile and shrug my shoulders, run my fingers along the counter he stands behind.

"I will make one waffle for you," he says, in lovely Belgian-French accented English. "A special waffle."

"Thank you." I smile. He steps from behind the counter and crosses to the door. He wears an apron to his knees but now I see he's also wearing shorts, and white socks with track shoes revealing shapely hairy legs.

"But first, we close," he says, and locking the door, turns the sign to 'Fermé'.

Walking past me, "My name is Albéric," he says, then opens another door and disappears. I crane my head, look through the doorway and see into the kitchen.

"You can be in the kitchen for watching, if you like," Albéric calls out to me. "The other staff has gone home."

So I saunter into the kitchen, stand just inside the doorway, slide my backpack off my shoulders. He stands beside a long stainless steel island bench and ladles waffle mix from a bowl onto a waffle iron. There are many waffle irons of different sizes and shapes positioned on a bench along a wall. But here he uses a small one-waffle version, heart-shaped, set up on the end of the island bench. The kitchen is spotless, the island bench in the middle cleared of everything bar the heart-shaped waffle iron.

"You are from Australia?" he says as he pulls the top of the waffle iron down and clamps it shut.

"Yes," I say, leaning against the doorway. He covers the bowl of waffle mix and places it inside a fridge.

"I was living in Sydney for two years. What's your name?"

"Paul."

The waffle iron pops and sizzles. "I like Aussie men," he says. Then stepping past me, he closes the door softly, cups his hand around my arse, and kisses me.

My cock is already leaking in my shorts and as his tongue slips into my mouth, he pulls his apron off and tosses it on a bench.

My arms wrap around his waist and he presses me against the island bench, tongue deep in my mouth, licking my teeth, my tonsils, my tongue. He drops to his knees, pulls down my shorts and jockstrap, and his mouth globs on my cock, deep throating it, all the way in, saliva slick, slathering the shaft, clasping my balls, pulling them as he sucks sucks sucks my cock hard, my trimmed pubes scratching his nose. His tongue wraps around my cockhead as he works it down his throat, and I sink back against the bench, surrendering control to him, sighing with pleasure, finally getting the attention my hormones and ego and penis need.

He stands up, grabs my meat and squeezes it hard, then reaches across to flick a switch on the waffle iron. Then he grabs my hips and spins me around, my groin hard against the island bench, and his shorts pulled down, presses his cock against my arse. The waffle iron stops its spluttering and popping at the other end of the bench, and he pushes my head down so my chest lies flat on the bench and my arse sticks out. Spitting on my hole, he pushes a finger past my sphincter. But it's a bit dry, so he opens the fridge and pulls out a large industrial size container of butter. Lid snapped off, he runs two fingers through it, rubs it between his fingers 'til it's spreadable and smears the melting butter on my hole. It feels smooth and slick and a little greasy, but his cock is hard and pressing his knob against my pucker, I open up and his meat slides in, butter and all.

Albéric is tall and rangy and so is his cock, long and muscly but not beercan thick, and these are the cocks I do best with. He works his pole deep inside me, a quick and instant rhythm, in and out and in and out and in and out and in and out, holding my arse hostage, and I push back against his hips, feeling his knob press up and in and against my guts. Oh man, his cock fills me up and I gasp and hunker down and push push push so it's deeper deeper deeper inside me. Fuck, mate! Where have you been the last three days?! I think. And he thrusts in deeper and my mouth gapes open, as if his cock is going to pierce my guts and cum directly in my mouth, sprog onto the bench in front of me.

He pulls out, spins me around again and pushes me back against the bench. He slaps the surface with his hand – "Your arse goes here," he orders – so I hoick my arse up onto the bench and he grabs my legs, pushes them up onto my stomach so my buttery hole is exposed and open. Cock slides back inside, to the hilt. Fuck, he can just keep it there, deep inside me, jammed up high, a little thrust every five seconds to remind my hole what it's there for: his cock's pleasure and my eye-rolling ecstasy.

My eyes glaze over as he withdraws, like a fencer's foil, a soldier's sabre, a swashbuckler's sword, then rams it back inside me – OOOPH! – and I cry out with pain and pleasure and he smirks, giggles, and repeats his attack: OOOPH! OOOPH! OOOPH! Fuck, my cries penetrate the air and roll across the ceiling. My fingers grip the edge of the island bench as I hold on as he fucks wrecks obliterates my hole. Oh my God … so intense and unexpected and fucking needed!

OOOPH! OOOPH! OOOPH!

He pulls out … a little too long … what have I done wrong? But he's just flipped the waffle iron lid open and flicks a heart-shaped waffle onto the benchtop with a finger. Pale and steaming, I wonder when –

OOOPH! OOOPH! OOOPH!

I want him to cum, to drench my hole with his pulsating seed, but I want him to hold off until my hole my heart my head can't take anymore, too. My back slips on the stainless steel as we rut, and looking up into his eyes, his cock a blur of action in out in out in out in out of my fuckhole, he suddenly slows, mouth open, sweat pouring down his forehead and he pulls out – don't pull out! – and grabs the heart-shaped waffle in his paw and holds back pulls back breathes in gasps then nuts shoots sprogs spunks his thick white load onto the waffle. He laughs, groans with the effort, breathes out, wipes his cummy cock on the crisp batter, and then pushes the waffle in my face.

"Eat!" he says.

I pull myself up, lean back on one elbow, take the jizz-waffle with my other hand and bite into it. My hips are still spread, so he slips two fingers inside my hole and with the expertise of a master, finds my prostate, starts rubbing it.

I breathe deep, chew on the waffle, as he rubs and rubs and rubs, devilish smile on his face. It's hard to eat a cum-waffle while your prostate's being rubbed scratched prodded fingered but fuck! I somehow manage it, legs spread, arse open, mouth full of soggy crunch. But then it gets too much and I breathe deep and moan and he rips the waffle from my clasp and bites into it, as the rubbing grows so intense that I grab my cock and jerk jerk gasp gasp jerk gasp jerk grind and clench my sphincter strangle his fingers as he licks the waffle, chugs it down, and the cum surges up through my cock, rushes up shoots out of the piss slit and covers blankets carpets my stomach and stomach hair and trimmed pubes and abdomen and navel and I throw my head back and my elbow collapses under me and I slump against the stainless steel bench.

And gaze up – blurry – at the ceiling.

"Ah, that … was magnificent," Albéric says, brushing waffle crumbs from his beard.

"Thanks for the topping," I say, sliding off the island bench. "And the butter."


The shop door closes softly behind me and I sling my backpack across my shoulders as I walk up the street. It's almost 8.00pm. With another 2 hours of sunlight left, that's enough time for another beer and more moules before restaurants close.

From my pocket, I pull out the business card Albéric gave me and read the writing he scribbled on the back: Sauna Macho, Rue du Marché au Charbon 106.

Or I could go there, save the beer and moules for tomorrow, and get a few more loads inside me instead.

# SANJEEV

# DADDY DIGS TRENCH

I am truly versatile and uniquely democratic. I'm not fussy. I'll fuck anything.

Though let me clarify – I don't have a type because I like all types.

Why limit myself?

Hairy, beefy, broad shouldered, older … I'll bend over against the urinal for you to slide your throbbing cock inside my fuckhole.

Nuggety and in a jockstrap? Happy for you to squat over my face while I eat your hole as you jerk off.

Younger and toned, with a wisp of hair around your balls? Will gladly sink to my knees and teach you the fine art of drinking piss straight from the tap. (Want an audience while class is in? Public parks are great for that on a dark and steamy night …)

30s or 40s, bearded and balding, with big swingers between your thighs looking to unload? More than content to provide the mouth that gets you off and the gullet that swallows your cumload.

But the ones where I unload my balls deep in their arseholes? Where I train their holes for deeper, harder, more penetrating pleasure … ?

They hold a … special place.

I just met a young fella who nails it for me: olive skin, big smile, desperate to spread his furry hole and take my thick veiny cock deep inside him.

He's good-looking, swarthy, an easy guy to get a hard-on over and fuck.

He's in the shower now … it's been interesting meeting up with him this first time …

Picture it: it's about 2.00pm. I hear brakes pulling into the bottom of the driveway. A hot young Indian dude jumps out of a courier van. It's really bright outside, and the sun beats down, heat reflecting in ripples off the concrete. I watch him through the window as he takes his time sauntering up the driveway, a large envelope in his hand. He knocks on the front door. I open the door to see him wearing tight tradie shorts that show off his bulging package and a white polo shirt with the courier company logo above his left nipple. Shirt unbuttoned and open at the top, chest hair curls underneath.

"Hey, mate," he says, with the trace of a lilt. He hands me the envelope. "You need to sign for it." He holds out a device. "Just use your finger to sign your name."

I work from home. So, I entertain at home, too. And I've been horny all day, half a hard-on raging in my shorts. I've been pulling my cock out while looking at spreadsheets; licking the pre-cum off my cockhead while flicking through unpaid invoices; shoving my fingers under my balls then pulling them out and sniffing their sweaty man scent then licking the taint off while I've been reading market reports. (Let me tell you, my balls smell funkier and taste saltier than any market report ever will!)

I'm all horned up with nowhere to dump my load.

"It's fucking hot," I say to the Indian dude. "You could probably use a cold drink. Can I get you a beer?"

A big grin splashes across his face. His chest expands to fill out his tight polo shirt, and his biceps strain against the short sleeves. And I reckon there's a stirring in his shorts, too.

I deepen my voice, talking from the base of my balls, and look him directly in his eyes. "Can you drink on the job?" And then, I joke: "Are you old enough to drink?"

"I'm 27, mate," he says, smiling, then adds: "Some rules are meant to be broken."

He leans against the kitchen doorframe, holding a beer in a stubby holder. I'm holding a beer in mine. I stand, weight pushed forward onto the balls of my feet, hips thrust out, growing cock straining against my shorts.

We talk, just shooting the shit but his eyes keep glancing at my protruding cock. And my eyes flick to his pecs, his biceps, his deep brown eyes, his smile, his thighs, his growing bulge.

Finally, he smiles, shakes his head and shifts his feet, places them further apart, and reaching down, adjusts his cock inside his shorts.

"You in a bit of trouble, mate?" I ask. "I can help you with that, if you want."

He looks at me. His tongue lolls on his bottom lip. I smile. I take the beer from his hand and place both our beers together on the counter next to the envelope. I grab his forearms and push them to his sides, press my chest against his erect nipples and pulling in close, force his mouth open with my tongue. His breath is beery and warm and his tongue wraps around mine. I breathe deep and smell hot-day man funk. Wrapping my arms around his waist, his warm body melts against mine. Our cocks are now rock hard inside our shorts, his rubbing mine through the fabric.

"I like your grey beard," he says, pulling away a little and caressing my chin with his hand.

"We need to fuck," I say.


He's lying naked on the bed. His chest hair descends to a dark crab trail across a flat stomach and down to a trimmed (but not too trimmed) bush – just how I like it. I push his knees up onto his chest. He moans. His arse opens up so there's a little give in it, tight but not too resistant. I lick my finger and slide it inside his hole. Crooking it, I rub his prostate. He gasps ... which is just how I like it.

I look down at his hole. His hole is hairy, so his arse hair sticks to my finger as I work it in and out, in and out, in ... and out ...

He moans again, then tightens his sphincter around my finger. I know my way around a man's arse, so I pull my finger out, spit on two of them, and slide two fingers back inside. In … and out … and in … and out. His hips rock with the rhythm of my fingers.

In and out. In and out. In out. In out. In out, in out, in-out in-out.

Fuck, this is exactly how I like it!

I'm imagining a summer afternoon rut, nipples erect and sweaty chest heaving, my tongue lost inside his mouth, my spurting cock buried deep inside his hot 27-year-old Indian courier arse, mouths gasping, sharp intakes of breath, plunging deeper as his hips press harder against me and I forget about spreadsheets and invoices and market reports and just fuck and fuck and fuck and fuck and fuck his delectable arse.

"Oh please," he whispers, catching his breath. "Please take your fingers out and put your cock inside and fuck me."

I want to fuck him. Fuck, I WANT to FUCK him. I want to push my thick cock deep inside and flood his arse with hot sticky cum. Yeah, I'm fully versatile but digging young trench makes me feel more fucking powerful than any other fuck task I enjoy.

And my cock is leaking big spreading drops of pre-cum.

But not just now, not just now with my fingers still doing the talking …

"Oh please, please fuck me," he says.

I push two more fingers inside him, up to the knuckle, twist them back and forth, round and round, grind them against his fuckhole, opening him up for my cock.

"Please, oh please, I need your cock," he groans.

I pull my fingers out of his arse and grip his ankles. My cock throbs just outside his sweet brown pucker. He looks up at me with imploring eyes. I press my cockhead against his hole.

"What d'you want, buddy?" I whisper.

"I want your cock!"

"Yeah?"

"Now!"

"When?" My voice is even deeper, coming even further from the base of my balls.

"Now!" he repeats. "Now! Fuck me now, oh please, please, fuck me now! Fuck me, Daddy!"

I drop one of his ankles – his free leg flaps about in mid-air, like it's suddenly lost its mooring.

*... Daddy?*

Bending forward, my hand clamps hard over his mouth.

He looks at me, head still.

I glare at him. "Shut the fuck up with this 'Daddy' shit!"

Eyes wide and wondering, he struggles to breathe under the grip of my hand.

"You gonna fuckin' stop?"

He nods.

"Daddy... DADDY? ... I'm not your fuckin' daddy."

He nods again, eyes *very* wide.

"You *really* gonna stop with this shit?"

His head bobs up and down like one of those dogs on the shelf in the rear window of a car.

I pull my hand away and grab his free ankle again.

And look down at my cock and see it looks like it's suddenly lost its mooring, too.

But his cock is hard – straining so hard! – you could crack rocks on it!

"What can I call you then?" he asks, licking his lips, head cocked, his mouth a wry smile. "I have to call you something."

I drop his ankles and sit back on my haunches.

I look into his eager-to-please face. I want him on his knees. I want him gagging on my cock. I want him slurping my piss, rimming my hole deep with his tongue and begging for my cum. I had some big plans in my head for this afternoon and a whole list of things I wanted to introduce him to and explore.

I've gotta give him something.

"Sir," I say. "Call me sir."

"Okay, sir," he says.

I like the sound of "sir". Cliché, yeah, but still: powerful and dominant and hard. And not fuckin' *Daddy*.

With one hand, I grip my thumb and index finger around his balls and stretch them, pulling the sack down and out. With the other hand, I push my fist against his hole. I want him to take my fist. I want to train that pucker to open up and take my fist up to the forearm. This is just the beginning.

He smirks.

"I will call you sir, sir. Just like you said, sir."

The grin on his face spreads almost as wide as I want to spread his arsehole.

"Please use your thick cock and fuck me, sir."

"Okay, I will," I say, "I will."

I grab both his ankles again and spread his legs wide. I press my growing cock against his hole. I'll use my thick cock and fuck you, certainly, I think. Yeah, but I have other plans, too ...

# PACKAGE DELIVERED

"A buddy is coming over this afternoon, sir, after work," Sanjeev says, his back to me, pouring boiling water from the electric kettle into a teacup. "He's coming over to fuck me."

Sanjeev replaces the kettle on its stand, and dunks a teabag, up and down, in the cup. The kitchen fills with the fragrance of musky, flowery, fruity Darjeeling. Since he moved in, the house smells have changed.

I watch his long, lean, dusky body as he dunks his teabag. His arse moves up and down, ever so slightly, but it really has a fucking life of its own, that arse. His butt cheeks are curvy, ripe peaches in his white jocks, and just above the waistband is a small patch of hair, dark and wispy. I want to sink to my knees behind him and nibble that hair with my teeth. Then pull out the leg elastic of his white jocks and slide my hand between his legs, rub his crack as the dunking slows, dip down to caress his hole as he spreads his feet on the floor so I can gain easier access (as the dunking stops), slowly push my finger inside, past his sphincter so I can rub his prostate, hard, harder as he sinks back onto my hand, as he moans, as he groans, as I make him late for work again ...

"Sanjeev, you don't need to –" I say, back in the moment.

"I must be honest and upfront, sir – no more sneaking around in my life."

What I started to say was he didn't need to call me 'sir' out of the bedroom. But since Sanjeev left his wife, it's all about "living my best life", "an authentic life", "MY life." That, and fucking men while he's out delivering packages as part of his courier job. And the more packages he delivers, the more workouts his package gets.

I pat him on the shoulder. "You don't have to call me 'sir' outside of the bedroom. We're housemates," I add, "you don't owe me anything except rent and common courtesy."

Though there are definitely fringe benefits.

"He is hung like a donkey," Sanjeev says, turning and sipping his tea. The slug in his jocks looks moist and muscly, poised for a hard day of action. "His cock looks delicious."

"You've tasted it?" I ask, assuming they met on his courier round.

"Only online. But tonight, it's the big night, sir." And he smiles over the rim of his cup. "I mean, not sir."


I meet Tony, the bloke with the delicious cock. Tony shakes my hand, clasping it in a firm grip. Handsome, older, gym-fit and on the tall side, green eyes, erect nipples, with a full head of grey hair and a short, neat grey beard and a mat of grey hair on a barrel chest poking out from behind his tank top. Big low-hanging bulge in his jeans.

"Good to meet you, mate," he says.

Fuckingly, ball-churningly, arse-tighteningly hot.

And the door shuts behind them as they disappear into Sanjeev's bedroom.


Since he left his wife and moved in temporarily, Sanjeev has taken over the kitchen. "My wife is a very modern woman, so she hates to cook," Sanjeev says. "But I like to cook. And I like cock, too."

So we have this arrangement. He usually cooks. I usually fuck him. Then we usually eat dinner.

So now I'm wondering what's going to happen about dinner tonight …

But I'm not hungry. I lie on my bed with a copy of 'Sharing Your Singlehood' on my lap. But the words are blurry and the book is fucking dull and there's a volcano in my trackpants. Plus, there's a share bathroom between my bedroom and Sanjeev's bedroom, and the door between my bedroom and the bathroom is open. And the door between Sanjeev's bedroom and the bathroom is shut.

I pull my cock out of my trackies – I'm freeballing, always ready for action – but it lolls there, half-interested, uncertain what I want to do with it.

Pushing my cock back inside my trackies, I toss 'Sharing Your Singlehood' aside, sneak through the bathroom and stand listening at Sanjeev's door. The doors are thin and not very sturdy, so it's not hard to hear what's happening on the other side. Though not a lot, I think.

Some muffled slurping noises. Breathing out and breathing in. Some slapping of skin. The splurge of lube from a bottle.

I lean over and press the toilet button. Half-flush.

Sounds of the filling cistern ease and I hear some soft words. Perhaps a chuckle. Maybe the squeak of a bed spring. What sounds like clacking knitting needles … but can't be!

I lean over and press the toilet button again. A more convincing full flush.

As the sounds of the filling cistern ease again, I jump back as the door opens. A tallish bloke with a full head of grey hair, neat grey beard and a mat of grey hair on a barrel chest with erect nipples stands in the doorway. It's Tony.

I'm so caught out I don't initially see the big piece of meat standing erect in front of him.

"Would you like to join us, mate?" he asks, lifting his balls up to give them some air. "Your mate says you might want to fuck him."

I've ripped off my t-shirt before I've left the bathroom and I've shucked off my trackies before I reach the side of the bed.

Sanjeev, naked, hard cock straining for his navel, leans over and whispers, "Show him how to fuck me, sir."

In a second, I'm on the bed, kneeling between Sanjeev's open legs. I push his knees onto his chest, and sliding my finger inside his fuckhole – he's already lubed up, thanks Tony – grab both his ankles and poise my cockhead outside his pucker.

"Please fuck me, sir," Sanjeev says. "Fuck me good."

Suddenly I'm a little self-conscious. This is part of our role play, and Tony the grey-haired god is watching us perform.

Cock poised to enter Sanjeev, I feel another hard cock pressing behind me, and warm breath in my ear. "I wanna fuck you good, too, son," Tony the grey-haired stud whispers.

It's an offer too good to refuse. I slide my cock into Sanjeev's fuckhole. To the hilt. Balls deep, as deep as I can push it, into his guts. He gasps, eyes wide, like I'm splitting him in two.

Then slowly pulling out, I feel Tony's thick greasy meat penetrate my pucker. I slide back as Tony pushes his cock forward, to the hilt, balls deep, as deep as he can push it, into my guts. I gasp and he wraps a muscly arm around me, pulling me close, his mat of chest hair against my back, his mouth in my ear. "Am I fucking you good, son?" he asks.

"Fuckin' oath, mate," I whisper. "Though don't call me –" I say, only to gasp as Tony's big meat presses even further, deeper, ramming one final millimetre before he pushes me forward, off his cock … and my cock dives into Sanjeev's fuckhole again.

"Sir," Sanjeev gasps, "you are definitely fucking me good."

I thrust my arse back onto Tony's meat. He pushes deep into me, impaling me, hips pushing me forward so my meat drives through Sanjeev's pucker and into his arse again. Sanjeev gasps. With Tony's arm clasped tight around me, and his cock embedded in my arse, I'm pulled back out of Sanjeev's hole and then pushed back in … Tony's thick cock drives me forward then his muscled arm pulls me back … then drives me forward deep through Sanjeev's pucker then pulls me back … then drives me forward deep through Sanjeev's pucker then pulls me back … it's like we're both topping Sanjeev.

I pull away and start fucking Sanjeev with shorter thrusts, Tony's cockhead just inside my fuckhole then just outside, just inside then just outside, inside outside, inside outside. Sanjeev is writhing on my cock, moaning with pleasure, spreading his hips wider so I can get my cock right up inside him. I lean over and kiss him, open his mouth with my lips, tongues lashing. He wraps his arms around me and pulls me further into his mouth, my cock deeper into his manhole.

"Sir," he gasps.

Then Tony signals it's time for a change by scooping his big arm around me and pulling me back against his hairy chest. "Time to get on your back, son," he breathes in my ear.

Sanjeev scoots across the mattress and I flop on my back next to him. Tony grabs my ankles, pushes my knees onto my chest and in a split second ploughs his meaty cock deep inside my guts. I can feel every millimetre of his fat cock busting my sphincter, his cockhead right up inside my fucktube, his balls clanging a fuckin' rainbow tune against my arse.

"Fucking you good, son?" he asks.

"Yes," I moan. "Yeah, oh yeah ..."

As Tony fucks me, ploughs me, grinds into me, slams his cock so far into me I think his cockhead's going to shoot a cumload in my mouth, and as I grunt with each thrust, he's pushing me towards the edge of the mattress. Sanjeev, ever thoughtful, nips around the side and edges his leaky cock at my mouth, then plunges past my lips. Fuck his pre-cum tastes so sweet on my tongue! Then with my head now hanging over the edge, he forces his cock down my throat.

I'm gagging at each end, my fuckhole spasming with desire and my mouth full with cock and pre-cum and sweat and ...

I kind of lose track. I'm in another fuckin' world, with cocks in both my holes and hot men all over me. I can see myself on the bed, bent up but sprawled apart as I take pleasure at either end, and two men take their pleasure with me.

Sanjeev breaks the spell. He drags his cock out of my mouth and with four quick jerks and then a determined pull on his cock, almost unsheathing the skin he pulls it back so hard, growwwwwwlls then shoots his big load across my lips, my nose, my cheeks, my chin, my tongue, as I rock back and forth with the force of Tony's pounding cock.

I lick my lips, panting for Sanjeev's manjuice inside me, scraping it across my face with my hands and licking his cum off my fingers.

Tony eases off ... his intense pistoning slows, and he looks deep into my eyes as he leans over me and nose close to my cheek, sniffs deep on my face. Planting his mouth on mine, his tongue sucks mine down, greedy for Sanjeev's cum.

Pulling back, he works up a slow rhythm, not taking his eyes off my face, both his big hands now pinning my arms down onto the bed, grinding his meat into my hole with strength and power and fucking purpose.

"That good, son?" he asks.

"Yes," I say, "that's pretty fucking amazing."

He grunts. His eyes roll back as his balls constrict. He stops in mid-grind, then thrusts his cock in balls deep .... and floods my fuckhole, shoots it full of cum, the manjuice pumping deep into me. "Fill me up," I say. My sphincter feels his cock pulse as ropes of hot cummy fuckjuice flow.

I wait for the pumping ... to ... ease ... off ... breathe out ... just as Tony pulls his cock out, opens up my deflated arsehole with his fingers, and dips his head between my legs.

"Fuuuuuck," he says. "That's five days' worth of cum I shot into you, mate."

Funny. It's 'mate' again now he's nutted.

He slides his fingers inside my fuckhole then holds them up, five days' worth of cum glistening as it drips down to his knuckles. He leans over, and I stick out my tongue, hoping to taste his hot fuckjuice and my funky arsejuice but he darts past my open mouth and slathers the juice across my cheeks and chin.

I can smell his cock and my arse on my face. He bends down and taking my cock in his hands, says "It's your turn now," and slowly runs his tongue around my knob.

Sanjeev, kneeling behind me on the bed, reaches over and pinches my nipples, hard. "Harder," I say. He pinches them harder and lifts them, tweaks them, twists them, hurting but hot. I start jerking my cock as Tony, grey head bobbing between my open legs, laps at my twitching, oozing hole with his silky tongue.

Soon I'm jerking out a rhythm, hand gripping cock, pulling back and forth, pre-cum and fuckjuice and spit as lube ... and just as I arch my back and breathe in for the money shot, Tony grabs my balls and yanks them down, and shoves two fingers in my open hole and grinds them against my prostate – FUUUUUCK!

I shoot so far my chin and neck and chest are covered with sweet, hot, creamy jizz. My head flops back on the mattress, exhausted, but my tongue can't resist licking my lips for one last hit of man protein, and I run my fingers across my chin and neck and chest, scooping up cum and sliding it in my hungry mouth.

Sanjeev leans down and whispers in my ear, "Thank you for saving the day, sir."

Tony leans down and kisses my sticky, cummy, deflating cock, then smacks his lips with pleasure and swallows. "'Til next time, mate," he says, and standing up, picks up his discarded jocks, wipes them on his cock and balls, and holding them to his face, sniffs long and hard.

# A CUP OF CUM

No more hot arse on tap, I think, as I watch Sanjeev shove a large box of his shoes into the back of his courier van.

No more dusky cock to fondle at 2.00am either, as I see him toss ten of his shirts on coathangers on top of the box of shoes.

No more mouth to fill with my knob and cum and kisses, I know, as he slides the van door closed with a metal perrrrrr-thlunk.

No more someone else cooking dinner every evening. No more someone to talk to when I want to shoot the shit. No more –

"I am very sad to be leaving your house, Paul," Sanjeev says, as he stands on the driveway beside his van, hanging his head.

I bow my head, too.

"I love our fucking," Sanjeev continues. "You have taught me so much about giving and receiving pleasure from a man. Even though, for the past few weeks, I have been off my game."

"Jeez mate, off your fuckin' game or what?!" I say, hand slapping my forehead. "You've gone from living and breathing cock 24 / 7 to … well, being a fucking nun! You sure you really wanna go back to your wife?"

"I don't want to … but I am her husband, so it must be me who is impregnating her."

I shake my head.

"My wife is a modern woman, she knows my circumstances, but she wants to have a baby."

I shake my head again. Maybe I'm a bit more cut up about this than I realised.

"I will get tested and then I will shoot my sprog into a cup and impregnate her. She knows modern life is not all roses and hearts."

And there you have it. End of argument. The promise of a baby wins.

I look at the blue blue so-fucking-blue sky. All reasoning has fallen on deaf ears. "Just remember, mate, if you need a place to stay, you can always stay here again."

"I will miss your hospitality," Sanjeev says. "And also your cock."

Yeah, I think, heart heavy inside my chest: I'm sure as fuck gonna miss your hot arse, too.


The smells in the house have changed now Sanjeev has moved out. No Darjeeling. No hing. No ghee.

And I am reminded of this when my mobile pings. 'I cannot cum without a man,' Sanjeev texts. 'I need your help.'

I throw aside the Business Activity Statement I am working on. Sanjeev's house is twenty-five minutes drive from mine, but I make it in twenty.

Sanjeev greets me at the side gate to his house, wearing his work uniform: tight tradie shorts that show off his bulging package and a white polo shirt with the courier company logo above his left nipple. Shirt unbuttoned and open at the top, chest hair curling underneath.

Wrapping his arms around me in a big hug, "My wife is on the other side of the house," he says. "She is waiting for my cum."

I breathe in his Sanjeev smells. I don't know what they are but they're him. I look into his dark sparkling eyes, and his handsome Bollywood movie star face. It feels good to be back inside Sanjeev's arms. "Fuck, it's good to see you, mate." I cannot wait to get my hands down his shorts.

"Now is the perfect time of her cycle to impregnate her," Sanjeev continues. "She is a modern woman, and modern women know these things."

I follow Sanjeev's bouncing arse around the side of the house to the back garden, mouth watering. He frowns as he looks towards the rear of the house, then opens the door to a garden shed. He ushers me in, shuts the door behind me, then locks it.

What can I tell you – it's a garden shed. Except Sanjeev isn't much of a gardener. Maybe no one in his family is.

But he's gone to some effort. A mattress covered with a sheet lies on the floor. And two old spidery lawnmowers, and pots and shovels and bags of fertiliser, have clearly been pushed aside to make room. Dirt and dust have been swept into a little pile in a corner.

"It is not very romantic, sir, but today it is more about getting down to the business."

This garden shed set-up makes me question how much Sanjeev's modern wife really knows.

"How we gonna do this?" I ask.

"It is mostly about collecting seed," he answers. "So I am thinking circle jerk. Then I will collect my sperm and give it to my wife."

I love a good circle jerk. But you need more than two fellas for that, and for me, the possibility of something harder to follow as added incentive as well: like cock in arse action, or "soggy biscuit" at the very least.

"What about if I fuck you, so you can jerk off and shoot into the cup," I suggest.

"Okay," Sanjeev nods.

I smile, and nod, too. "Where's the cup?"

Sanjeev reaches behind a dusty bottle of poison and pulls out an opaque plastic cup, one of those inexpensive ones you buy as a set of six for $2.00 at a cheap shop. It doesn't look very scientific or biological, though at least it's not china with pink flowers around the edge.

"My wife has a turkey baster with her," Sanjeev says, reading my mind. "She will use that to inseminate herself from the cup."

This whole thing sounds so … so-so. I'd say this but I don't have the heart to tell him. Plus, I just want to get my cock sliding inside his arse. And I'm always the take-charge one.

"If I don't fuck you soon, mate, I'll be losing my fuckin' boner."
I grab his hips and pull him towards me. He chuckles, and we kiss,
soft lips on soft lips, hot tongue probing hot tongue, wet and juicy
and warm. It feels good to be back inside Sanjeev's mouth.

Sanjeev pulls away and like lightning, is lying on his back on the
mattress, shorts, jocks, and polo shirt in a bundle on the floor. The
cup lies beside him on the mattress.

I rip off my own clothes and am soon kneeling between his open
legs, finger finding his hole.

Tongue lolling on his lips, Sanjeev coos, "I did come prepared,
sir."

"Yes, I can tell." I stick two fingers, then three fingers, inside his
hole, crooking them to rub his prostate. It's so slippery inside his arse
it's a wonder my fingers can gain any traction. He must have emptied
a 5-litre bottle of lube in his arse!

The bugger is, I don't like it too slippery, I like it sticky. I can
fuck an arsehole that's really slippery, no probs, but cumming inside
it? My cock needs something to grind against.

And I'm getting mixed messages here … let's circle jerk but I
came prepared with an arse full of lube?

"Fuck me, sir."

So I do. I slide my rock-hard cock inside Sanjeev. It feels good to
be back inside his hole. He hooks his legs over my shoulders as I lean
into him, quickly working up a rhythm, in – out – in – out – in – out
– in – out – looking him in the eyes – in – out – in – out – pelvis
rocking back and forth – in – out – in –

"Oh, I have missed your cock, sir," Sanjeev whispers.

"I've missed your hole too, buddy," I say. "Shouldn't you be
jerking off into the cup?"

"Yes, but I am enjoying your fucking."

Leaning in, I kiss him again, just lightly, soft and giving, to
remind his lips my lips are here too, and I am totally with him again.

Sanjeev picks up the cup and sits it on his stomach. But his eyes
are closed, lost in my cock and his hole, and his cock is hard and

leaking but his hands rest on his stomach. The cup rocks in rhythm with our fucking.

In-and-out and breathing hard and closed eyes and licked lips and looking down and over him and in-and-out and enjoying each moment – enjoying the moment – and the moment – and the moment – and the moment – and the moment – and the moment – and the moment – and the moment – and the moment –

This cock and hole reunion is great but I know it's not going to get me off. Too much lube. Slipping and sliding.

– and the moment – and the moment –

Sanjeev, eyes still closed, reaches over and touches his cock.

– and the moment – and the moment –

His boner is so hard every thrust I make into his hole sends his cock bouncing against the dark crab trail on his dusty skin. Like a fucking spring.

"Oh, Paul," he says. "I mean, sir –"

"Call me Paul, mate," I say between a breath and a thrust and another breath and another breath. "That's my name."

I shake my head. Stop. Pull out. Sanjeev's legs fall off my shoulders and he looks at me, concerned.

"It's not you, Sanjeev," I say. "It's me. I can't … "

"What?"

I point at his hole. "It's too fuckin' sloppy in there!" I say. "There's no friction!" I kneel up, my cock pointing over his crotch. "I'll have to jerk off."

This was a bad idea, I'm thinking, but Sanjeev makes me so fucking horny and hot and I wanted to share more good times with him.

I start pulling my cock, looking Sanjeev in the eye. Sanjeev starts pulling his cock, looking me in the eye. My lip curls and his grin hardens into a grimace and we're pulling and glaring at each other. I press against his open thighs, leaning into him, eye contact, watching his face as he strains and jerks. He lowers his eyelids, he's so fucking sexy, and I jerk and jerk and jerk and he jerks and jerks and jerks –

"Fuck me, sir," he says. "Fuck me, Paul," he jerks. "Fuck me, sir. Fuck me, Paul."

"I am fucking you, Sanjeev," I growl and jerk. "I'm fucking you now," I jerk. "My cock is fucking deep inside your hole."

My balls are churning and I'm almost squeezing my cock I'm jerking so hard, pulling the skin back, working the shaft, my thighs thrusting against Sanjeev, pushing his legs wider apart, splitting his hole open.

Sanjeev looks at me with hot, yearning eyes. And spasms. He clutches at the cup, fumbling to set it in the right position.

The sap shoots up my cock and I'm ready to burst.

Sanjeev groans and cums, the cup in a position to collect –

And I cum, shooting over Sanjeev's pulsating cock and straight into the waiting cup.

It's shooting up my cock again and straight into the cup.

Out of my cock and into the cup again.

Sanjeev gasps as he's cumming and I growl as I keep shooting over him and onto and near and into the cup. I'm scoring holes-in-one and Sanjeev is going wide.

"But ..." he says.

I shudder and sit back, cock still hard between my legs, proud and red and leaking, exhaustion on my fucking face.

Lying back, Sanjeev groans, shakes his head, his cockhead wet but his face telling a different story.

He sits up, wipes cum from the side of the cup with his finger and scrapes it into the cup. Peering inside, "Whose is it?" he asks.

"I dunno," I say. I take the cup from his grasp, look inside. "I mean, sprog is sprog is sprog."

"Is it your sprog, Paul, or is it my sprog?" Sanjeev's eyebrows are somersaulting, his eyes in clear distress.

I dip my finger into the cum and lick the cum off with my tongue. "Tastes good," I say. And upending the cup, stick my tongue inside. Whosever it is, warm jizz slides into my mouth. "Good vintage," I add, "whatever the year." And swallow.

Sanjeev groans, falls back onto the mattress, his hand covering his eyes.

"I didn't want to waste it," I explain, licking my lips. "And you couldn't give it to her anyway," I add. "You can't impregnate your wife with what might be my cum."

"I must return to work," Sanjeev says, clutching at his clothes.

I push his hand down to stop him. "Gimme some time and we can do it again, mate."

Sanjeev sits up and glares at me. "Next time do not be so greedy, Paul. Leave the cup for my cum and please shoot your cum in my mouth or in my arse."

My head nods. Reaching down, I cup his balls in my hand. He startles at my touch, but sits there, still.

I really want to kiss him, mouth on mouth, soft lips on soft lips, take him back to another place ...

But I smile at him instead. "I'm just keeping your boys warm, Sanjeev," I say, "until Round 2."

# VIAGGIO
## IN
# ITALIA

# THREE COINS
# IN MY ARSEHOLE

Fuck, I love travel! It's about the 3Fs – foreign food, foreign friends, and foreign fucks.

Picture it – it's late May and the final day (and the final race) of the Giro d'Italia is tomorrow. And Rome is filled with men in tight, arse-hugging, calf-revealing, thigh-caressing, bulge-exposing, cycling shorts.

And I'm just one of them. (Mine are white, with stitching that nips across my cockhead – I dress to the left   and highlights my cut knob. If I stand with my hips pushed forward and really strain against the lycra, you can see the thick veins in my cock pop.)

It's difficult not staying hard all day when hot fuckers in tight shorts are milling around you. And with the crowds and the craziness and a country filled with such hot men anyway (and Rome is an incredibly sexy city), there's a lot of bumping (and grinding) and looking and gazing and light touching and catching glimpses and lingering gazes and … swelling glands.

Now, if you got a small package, cycling shorts will only emphasise your small-ish gift. If you got a medium-sized package, especially if your cock is long, then cycling shorts will do you proud, and there's many a cyclist who's picked up because his medium-sized cock and knackers have promised a nutritious diversion. (Plus, when you're lean, your cock always looks bigger!)

But when you're packing some serious meat in your cycling shorts, when your bulge rests almost on your bike's handlebars, no one's gonna look you in the face. Everyone's too busy staring at your meal ticket.

And that's just what I was doing as I stood in the Piazza di Trevi beside my bike with my own white bulge growing, surrounded by hundreds of tourists and 300,000 litres of water gushing in the Fontana di Trevi, the throb of my own pulse racing through my head and my heart and my cock.

I was staring at a young bloke's prominent light blue bulge.

It was late afternoon. He was lean and toned and tanned, a serious cyclist. And I was horny as fuck.

Blue bulge guy – let's call him Antonio, I never did catch his name – stood with his bike leaning against a wall. The piazza was crazy with rushing water and tourists tossing coins into the water and making wishes and snapping photos.

And I was ready to toss something else.

Antonio's dark soulful gaze searched my face. His eyes flicked to my bulge.

I pushed my hips out further, my cock a missile ready to launch.

Antonio smiled, dark eyes crinkling. He rubbed his short beard with his hand, cocked his head, and still meeting my gaze, slowly turned his bike, helmet dangling from the handlebars, towards a side street. A split second later he looked over his shoulder to see if I was following him.

I reached down and adjusted my cock. Men do that all the time in Italy, they're hard-wired to reach for their cocks at least once every two minutes. Antonio reached down and adjusted his cock, too.

Grabbing the handlebars of my bike, I wove along the edge of the crowd, watching Antonio's pert arse as he pushed ahead of me. And then he stopped.

Another cyclist in yellow bike shorts joined him, standing close, talking in his ear, bike parallel to Antonio's.

I leaned my bike against my hip, looked at the fountain and the crowd and the water.

The two men continued talking. Longer faces, aquiline noses. Antonio was younger, short dark hair. The other bloke – let's call him Lorenzo, I never did catch his name – in his 40s, had a shaved, tanned head, glossy like a cockhead, foreskin pulled back, ready to blow. And a short goatee.

(What is it with me and facial hair?)

Lorenzo looked at me, smiled, nodded.

Two mates? Boyfriends? Father and son?

Cock bursting in my lycra, balls churning pre-cum, I followed as they slowly walked their bikes out of the Piazza di Trevi.

Antonio looked over his shoulder at me. Lorenzo looked over his shoulder, too.

I nodded and smirked. I'm coming, fellas, I'm coming, I wanted to call out.

Their pert arses, rhythmic in their bike shorts, led me down the Via delle Muratte.

Controlling my excitement with deep breathing, I watched the two men stop at the corner of Vicolo delle Bollette.

I peered in a gelato shop window. Which flavour should I ask for? Mancum? Balljuice? Piss and Pre-cum Ripple?

A third bloke with a bike stood talking with Antonio and Lorenzo. Older again, lean and tanned and toned, longer face and aquiline nose, short grey hair and beard, green cycle shorts, a real silver fox. He looked at me.

I looked away. Mancum gelato, please. Looked back.

The silver fox – let's call him Sergio, I never did catch his name – smiled. A genuine smile. I smiled back.

The men and their bikes turned right into Vicolo delle Bollette.

And I turned right into Vicolo delle Bollette.

The noise of bike wheels on pavement returned as the fountain and tourists and crazy noise receded. And I heard thumping in my chest.

The men stopped at a patterned wrought iron door and pulling a key from the back of his cycling jersey, Lorenzo the middle guy unlocked it, pushing the door open. They filed their bikes inside, focussed on their task.

Three mates? A throuple?

Grandfather, father and grandson?

I admit – that last possibility got my cock grinding the most.

Sergio the silverfox stuck his head through the doorway and smiling, said, "Presto."

I wheeled my bike through the door. Lorenzo pushed the door closed behind me and it locked shut.

It was dark, an entryway to … what? I couldn't tell. Through holes in the wrought iron door I could see the pavement and buildings opposite, but as hands felt their way up inside my jersey and pulled down my bike shorts, I didn't fucking care. Three hot men had led me into this dimly lit entryway and I trusted they knew what they were doing.

Sergio's probing tongue opened my mouth. I smelt sun and heat on his beard and tasted man on his tongue. Drawing me in, he slid his arm around my waist and pressed his fat hard-on against me. Tongue lashing mine, entwined around it, he sucked on it, nibbled my lips and whispered something in Italian, something fucking hot and sexy.

Sergio stood back and Lorenzo nipped in, dipping to my nipples, working them with his teeth and his pinching fingers, squeezing them, biting them, nipping them, teeth and tongue nibbling around the edge then pulling them tight and stretching them out. I held onto his shaved head, licked his slick pate and cried with pleasure, wondering what Antonio, who was standing off to the side, would do.

As Lorenzo worked my nips, Antonio crouched behind me and slid his wet fingers along my crack. I widened my stance, bent my knees and stuck my arse out. His wet fingers found my hole, spread it open, digging inside. Lorenzo yanked on my nipples, and I gasped loud enough for passersby to hear, I'm sure. Sergio planted his mouth on mine again, his tongue engorged, silencing any moans or cries I made.

Antonio said something in Italian and stood up. I heard the squelch of lube and felt a wet, cool, slimed-up finger on my hole again. Lorenzo released my nips and Sergio hugged me around the neck and pulled me down, so my arse was more exposed and my chest and shoulders were cradled by his arms. Gripping my hips, Antonio slowly edged his young, hard cock through my pucker. His cock was thick, even meatier than I expected but my hole relaxed and opened up, glad to finally have the cock it needed. I gripped onto Sergio's shoulders as Antonio worked his meat into me, steamed up a steady rhythm, fucking me, drilling me, grinding his cock in my arse, the top of his legs slapping my cheeks as he drove, pummelled, slammed his meat into me.

As I rocked between Antonio's pounding and Sergio's arms, Lorenzo stroked his own meat. Lorenzo smiled, said something to Antonio in Italian, and then the young buck gave two massive thrusts and a final ram and burying his cock balls deep, groaned and shot his load into me.

I stood still, feeling the intensity of his cock pumping manjuice into my fuckhole, ring gripping cock, not wanting to waste any cum … four … five … six … seven pumps of sprog, all to the sound of his heavy breathing.

He pulled out and leaned against the wall, chest heaving. Grabbing my arm so I twisted around to see his face, he leaned forward and kissed me, his tongue in my mouth, his breath warm on my face, his beard and moustache smelling of sweat and spit and my arse.

Being the youngest of the trio, I hadn't expected Antonio to last long … and as his tongue explored the back of my throat, faces smacked together, I wondered what the trio's next trick would be.

Then I felt Antonio's finger prodding my hole, pushing something small and cool inside it.

I pulled away and wiped my mouth, panting.

Sergio seized the moment and pulling out his thick cock from his green shorts, pushed my head down towards his crotch. My hole still tingling from Antonio topping me, the prickle of Sergio's shaved pubes was a shock. They were probably grey, I thought, but his sweaty cock was girthy and tasted of so much sweet pre-cum, I lapped it up. Sergio held my head and throat-fucked me, a steady rhythm, in out, in out, in out, in out. And bent over, that's when I saw a young guy through the holes cut in the door, standing on the pavement in Vicolo delle Bollette, pulling his bulge through his orange cycle shorts. He was saying something in Italian though not very loud, and Lorenzo hissed at him through the door. Looked like orange bulge wanted to come in. The heated conversation ended and orange shorts and his throbbing mound disappeared.

I still had Sergio's cock buried deep in my mouth. He grabbed the back of my head and pulling me towards him, pushed his cock deeper inside me. The older fella certainly knew how to take control, intense and long stuffing of his cock in my mouth, me gagging and spluttering but not being able to (and not wanting to) pull away. His balls slapped against my chin, so I reached up and grabbed them both, pulling them down. He moaned, a low cry deep from the base of his sack, and then stopped ... stopped ... stopped ... held my head tight, my nose squashed against his shaved pubes ... then gripped my ears just as ropes of hot cum filled my mouth. I pulled back on my heels just in time so I could taste it on my tongue, creamy and sweet and a reward earned, before swallowing it, gulping it down, sliding it down my throat and down, deep down into my guts.

Standing up, I wiped my mouth, panting.

Then I felt Sergio's hand on my arse. Slowly prodding my hole with two fingers, it twitched as he slid something small and cool inside it. I wanted to know what he'd pushed into me but then I saw Lorenzo pulling his hard cock. He had so much thick foreskin, I wanted to nibble it, bite it, probe my tongue around the head and chew on the snackable manhood, finger it and stretch it out. Sergio had filled my mouth with cum and Antonio had filled my arse with cum. How would Lorenzo use me?

Sergio said something in Italian and he and Antonio each grabbed one of Lorenzo's shoulders and shoved him to his knees. Lorenzo slurped my cock into his mouth then grabbed my hands and slapped them around his bald head. I pulled his head towards my cock and pushed deep inside his mouth. This was not what I was expecting. But he serviced me well, licking around the head, grabbing my balls and pulling them down to steady me, pushing his tongue into the piss slit, spitting on my cockhead and sliding his lips along my shaft.

While Lorenzo worked my cock over, Antonio and Sergio stroked their fucksticks, pinched my nipples, slapped my face lightly in encouragement, pointed at Lorenzo's solid cock sucking, licked up their own leftover cockjuice. But they were all so dominant, this trio, so ... macho Italian, that Lorenzo sucking my cock with such dedication was puzzling. Expert, hell yes, but puzzling.

Lightly flicking his tongue around my cockhead, jerking my cock with his free hand, I felt my sap rising and decided, well, fuck it! I have to cum some time. And so I did, gripping my glutes, thrusting deeper into his mouth, balls churning out wads, scads, great streaks of hot sticky mancum, filling his mouth, him lapping with his tongue, gulping man protein, chugging it all down, not wasting a single sweet drop.

Pulling away, Lorenzo wiped his mouth, panting. Then standing, he drew close to me, smiled, and opened his mouth wide. "Buh-UUuurrrp!"

So that's his deal – a cum burp in my face. Warm and cummy and ... well earned.

"Putano," he said to me.

Darting behind me, he found my hole with expert speed, and prodding it open with his fingers, slid something small and cool inside it.

The door unlocked.

Light shone through as the door opened. Adjusting their cocks back inside their bike shorts, the three men grabbed their bikes, wheeled them outside ... and door closing behind them, were gone.

Stepping out of my bike shorts, I flung them across my bike and squatted on the floor. Tensing my muscles, I pushed Antonio's cum out of my arsehole onto the gritty tiles. Sitting in a pool of cum were three coins. I picked them up, looked at them in the light through the door. They were three gold coins. Three 10-cent coins; ten cents for each cumload. I wiped each coin on my leg and popped them in my mouth, rolling them in my spit with my tongue to lick them clean. They'd need to be clean before I drilled holes into them and hung them on a chain around my neck.

Shorts on, coins pocketed in the back of my jersey, I pushed the door open and wheeled my bike into Vicolo delle Bollette. A young bloke, 20s, lean and toned and tanned and wearing orange cycling shorts and a tense expression, stepped towards me.

"You fuck me," he said. "You have a hotel room?"

Did the entire Rome cycling fraternity want to have a crack at my cock and holes?

"No mate, I'm fucked," I said, shaking my head.

"Yes, you top me, please," he said. "I will follow you."

I wheeled my bike towards Piazza di Trevi, wondering about my versatility. Love being fucked by older guys, love topping younger guys, love piss and cum, pretty well up for (almost) anything. Reconciling all of these roles can be interesting, as they're so diverse, and they're all me.

Maybe I really am just a whore.

Orange shorts wheeled his bike beside me. "Where is your hotel?" he said. "We walk there together."

I stopped, and looked at his long handsome face, aquiline nose, pale blue eyes, curly light brown hair. He grabbed his crotch in his orange shorts and adjusted his cock.

And I felt a stirring in my shorts, imagined parting his pert cheeks with my hard cock, listening to his moans of pleasure. And maybe if I fucked his mouth and shot a sprogload down his throat, he'd cumburp in my face … ?

"Okay, I'll fuck you," I said. "But let's talk on the way first."

# FOLDS OF FORESKIN

"My name is Ottavio." Stepping out of his orange cycle shorts, his long thick cock bounced between his thighs, folds of foreskin bobbling on the end.

"I'm Paul," I said, eyes glued to his tasty foreskin. Then I did the polite thing and looked into his pale blue eyes set above high cheekbones. "Or Paolo."

"Paolo or Paul?" Ottavio asked, lifting his balls up and scratching underneath. "Which is your name?" He pushed his fingers under his nostrils and sniffed.

"Paolo. In Roma."

"Eh, what happens in Roma, it stays in Roma." Ottavio smiled. He tossed his orange cycle shorts over his bike resting against the wall, then pulled his orange jersey over his head and threw that on the bike, too.

I was right. As we'd talked and wheeled our bikes back to the Hotel Scenario on Vicolo delle Ceste, I'd wondered if his nipples were pierced. He had small gold studs in both. I love pierced nipples. I prefer big rings that rock in rhythm while you're fucking, but studs will do at a pinch. (I don't have pierced nipples myself, but one day ...)

I pulled off my jersey, removed the three 10-cent coins I'd earned earlier in the Vicolo delle Bollette, and placed them on the bedside table. Shucking off my bike shorts, I sat on the edge of the bed to –

"I will help you," Ottavio said. Kneeling on the floor, he pulled off my shoes, then peeled off my socks, placing them neatly on the floor at the end of the bed.

He had the longest eyelashes. They cast a shadow hallway across his cheeks when he looked down.

Lifting my arm up, I sniffed my armpit. "I need a shower," I said.

"No," Ottavio said, looking up at me. "First you fuck me, then take a shower, then again you fuck me."

"You don't mind if I don't have a shower first?"

He knelt up and pulling up my arm, stuck his nose into my pit and breathed deep, then licked it, sucking the hair. My armpit was ripe …

"No," he replied. "Fuck me. Then we take a shower. Then fuck again."

"Dunno if I've got the juice to fuck you twice, mate."

He scrambled onto the bed and positioned himself on all fours, arse facing me. He had a disk, a round stopper, where his arsehole should be.

Looking close-up at the end of what was a buttplug moored in his hole, I wondered if I had the juice to fuck him even once! After my encounter with the three musketeers near the Fontana di Trevi, I was surprised I'd been able to walk back to the Hotel Scenario at all!

Still, that muscled arse – not an ounce of fat on that thing – and his lean, toned thighs and calves, hole sticking out. Maybe I had enough sap in me to rise to the occasion.

As I stood by the bed and caressed the mounds of his butt, he looked at me with playful eyes, and said, "I need my hole to be filled 24 / 7."

I smiled, started pushing lightly on the buttplug with my fingers.

"Every hour," he added, "every day."

I gripped the edge of the plug and pulled on it, just a little.

"So it is ready always and open."

Pushed the plug back in. "How do you know the other blokes?" I asked.

"What?"

Fingers tapping on the stopper, sending little waves of expectation through his ring and hole and stomach and all five senses.

70

"How do you know those three men, Ottavio? I saw your cock in your orange shorts through the holes in the door."

"They, I don't know so much," he said. His ring tightened around the plug. "They are always together, always cruising. They call them 'The Fucking Priests'."

"Priests?" I looked over at the three 10-cent coins lying on the bedside table. That might explain their charity.

Ottavio nodded. Looked at me over his shoulder. Bit his bottom lip.

I nipped around to his face, lifted my left armpit. He pushed his nose into it and I grabbed the back of his head, holding it deep in my pit. He huffed long and hard, inhaling my sweaty stench. Looking under him, I watched a sticky stream of pre-cum drop through his foreskin onto the sheet.

He nodded at my right armpit. I grabbed his head again and shoved it into my other armpit. He licked the sweat, gripped my pit hair with his teeth, pulled, dribbled spit down my pit and onto the sheet.

Then pulling away, he closed his eyes, tensed his stomach, and shot out the buttplug from his arse. It bounced on the mattress and lay glistening between his calves, black and glossy with lube and arsejuice and sweat, about 20 cm long, flaring near the stopper to keep his cavern enlarged. It lay like a secret missile, winking and demanding attention.

"Make me your putano," he whispered.

Grabbing the plug, I shoved it back inside his hole. He flinched. I pulled it out and shoved it back in, even harder. "Yes," he groaned, sticking his arse out further. I grabbed it back, and rammed it in. "Sì." Grabbed it back and rammed it in. Grabbed it back, rammed it in. Grabbed it back, rammed it in. "Eh sì, sì." Grabbed it, rammed it. Grabbed it – "sì" – rammed it. Grabbed, rammed. Grabbed, rammed. "Sì." Grabbed, rammed. Grabbed, rammed.

He lowered his arms and lay his head and shoulders on the mattress, arse stuck out at a sharper angle. I pushed the plug slowly into him again, nudging it from underneath with the heel of my palm in short thrusts, knocking it against his prostate. Knocking it. Knocking it. Knock. Knock. Knock knock knock knock knock knock knock knock knock knock knock.

"Sì. Sì. Sì sì sì sì sì sì." Ottavio moaned long and loud. "Sssìiiìiiiìiiiìiiiìiiiì." Gasping, his eyes rolling back in his head, his mouth open, he groaned and sighed and whimpered.

Knock knock knock knock knock knock knock knock knock knock knock. Fuck, it was like my cock was digging into him.

Then Ottavio pushed back up on his hands and said, "Stop, please. Use your cock now."

I ripped the buttplug out and Ottavio flipped over onto his back, pushing his knees up onto his chest.

I stood the buttplug on the bedside table, then grabbing some lube, slicked it along my cock, rubbed it in, and kneeling between his spread legs, poised my meat outside his gape.

Ottavio's eyes grew wide, his mouth wider.

Bent over him, I slowly slid my cock inside. My cock is meaty, veiny, girthy … there are longer cocks and fatter cocks but – true – mine looks like it's been sculpted. Ottavio gripped my arse with his hands, forcing my butt and my hips and my cock deeper in his guts. And my cock fit inside him so perfectly, so snugly, touching the sides and reaching deep deep deep into his soul.

"Eh," he cried. "Sì. I am a Ph.D student and my thesis is about the US invasion of Sicily in 1943."

I pulled out then drove back balls deep into his willing anus.

"Fuck me like a G.I. invading Sicily."

I pulled out.

Stopped.

Ottavio looked at me, grabbed my cheeks to pull me into him.

"Do you think I'm American?"

His fingers twisted my nipples. "Sì. Now fuck me."

I sat back on my heels.

Fingers stopped twisting my nipples.

"Sorry to disappoint you, mate, but I'm not American, I'm Australian."

He looked at me with his pale blue eyes. "Eh, I am not so good about accents."

"If it's a deal breaker, then we'd better stop." But I did position my cockhead against his hole. And I still hadn't nibbled and sucked and eaten that delectable foreskin.

Ottavio smiled. "I don't waste a good fuck. Fuck me like you are a —"

But I clamped my hand over his mouth, to prevent the cardinal sin of him saying "kangaroo" or "koala".

And I kept it clamped as I slid into him again, deep, filling his space, watching his pale blue eyes widen again, as I built up a fucking rhythm: cock and hole, fuckstick and fuckhole, manpole and manhole, joyrider and tunnel of love.

I slid my hand off his mouth, caressed his high cheekbones, traced his aquiline nose, brushed his lips. He bit my finger, lightly, playfully.

"It's so hot, it's so hot, it's so hot," he whispered, chanting, a mantra, as his hips rocked back and forth with each willing, gentle thrust of my cock. Looking up into my eyes, he fondled my cheek with his hand and pouted a small kiss. "Amore mio," he said.

I know what that means.

It was the heat of the moment.

I stepped up my pace. I really wanted to cum in his mouth and then have him cum burp in my face, sweet and acrid and intimate and piggy. I REALLY wanted that. But then he tightened his ring around my cock and I didn't want to disappoint him either. I leaned down and kissed him, soft lips on soft lips. He opened his mouth and his silky wet tongue licked mine, then withdrew, enticing mine inside his.

I kissed him, deep and intimate. His hand caressed my back, cooing as we kissed, like he was opening up in front of me, under me, and I was opening up inside him, too. I breathed out, into his mouth, and he turned his head and moaned as I breathed across his face. I licked his eyebrow, nibbled his earlobe, tongued his ear, all while slowly penetrating his hole, sliding in and sliding out, licking his face, blowing on his closed eyelids and long eyelashes, enjoying the slow rhythm of my cock and his hole and my cock and his hole and my cock and his hole and my cock ...

(Fuck, I could fall in love with this guy ...)

Ottavio opened his mouth again, a gasp, arching his back and pushing his pelvis against my grinding meat. "Fuck fuck fuckfuckfuck ... me," he moaned, deep breathing.

"You want my cum?" (I could cancel my plans to visit Venezia and Firenze and Genova ...)

"Yes ... sì ... "

"Now?" (I could spend the next few weeks in Roma instead, just fucking and getting to know you and fucking ...)

"... yes. Yes yes yes."

I pushed my hips, levering his pelvis up and over so my cock could get as deeeeeeep into him ... his body curled under me, his face open and wanting and tensing and expectant ... and I gave him three momentous slams – SLAM – SLAM – SLAM – and then "Aaaaarghhhh!" – I shot – shot – shot my load – "Fuuuuuuuuck!" – deep ... deep ... deep ... deep ... deeeep inside him.

I fell back on my knees. Ottavio's hips and pelvis and cock rolled back with me.

He opened his mouth, then pulled me down over him and kissed me, on my chin, on my nose, on my mouth, on my open lips, tongue lunging in so fucking deep and long and probing and needy and sweaty and intense and insane.

My heart was thumping in my ribcage, sweat soaking my skin, dripping off my face and my pecs. Ottavio caressed my cheek, licking my sweat off his fingers then touching my sweaty shoulders then fingers into his mouth and my sweaty collarbone then in his mouth and my sweaty nipples then his mouth, sweat and saliva and kissing me then my mouth and his lips and my lips then his tongue and fuck! my tongue, too ...

My eyes focussed on his eyes, half-closed, fuzzy, ready to –

"Leave your cock in me," he whispered. "May you please pass me ..." and he nodded towards his buttplug. "Don't come out, stay in," he insisted, and clutched my butt.

I reached across and somehow grabbed the buttplug.

Ottavio took it from my grasp, slicked his tongue all over it, pulled away from me and gripping his sphincter tight, pushed the buttplug back inside his hole. Pulling me down to kiss me, he said, "You are saved inside me."

Later. Quite a while later. After talking and kissing and touching, after Ottavio saying he would save his orgasm for Round 2, we were showering. Hot water over our heads and backs and (pierced) nipples and down our legs and soap suds under his balls and under my balls and lathering up our cocks and playing and feeling his hole … except still the damn buttplug kept its mooring in Ottavio's arse. He must've had ERC – Extreme Rectal Control.

I cupped Ottavio's cock in my palm and did what I'd been longing to do since he'd undressed.

Licking the tip of my finger, I held his cock upright and ran my wet finger around the inside of his foreskin, stretching it out and up, pulling it back, running my finger back inside it, slowly round and round. I pulled the skin up 'til his cockhead disappeared, bent down and stuck my tongue inside, licked within the foreskin then pulled it back, tonguing his piss slit. Grabbed the foreskin and stretched it up again then spat a gob down it, slipped it around with my finger, pulled it out and stuck two fingers inside. Stretched it up and held the end closed and tugged, then opened it again and pushed my rock-hard penis up to his, docking, opening the foreskin and slipping my cockhead inside, knobs pressed together.

Completely lost in my play, Ottavio said, "You like your new toy."

"It's so sexy," I said.

He pulled his cock away, aimed at the floor, and shot a warm jet of piss on my feet.

My hand snatched his cock and squeezed the end of it, stopping any further flow.

"I'm not gonna waste any of that, mate," I said. Dropping to my knees, I directed his cock at my open mouth, loosened my grip, and clamped my lips around the foreskin and head as Ottavio's piss resumed its flow.

As warm water from the shower flowed over my head and shoulders and back, the warm piss flowed into my willing mouth, swirled over my tongue, down my throat, and poured warm and salty into my guts. It was ages since I'd had a stomach full of piss. Damn, I needed it, filling me up, recycling another man's resources, saving on hydration, pigging out.

(It's funny: when I'm being fucked, I wonder what it's like being the Top, and when I'm Topping, I wonder what the bottom's cock would feel like in my hole. But when I'm drinking piss, I just want to drink more piss!)

Ottavio clasped my ears as he leaned into me, piss continuing to flow. I gave 100% to chugging it down. It was a long stream, warm and bitter but satisfying. Glug glug glug chug chug chug. When he finished, when the final bursts trickled into my mouth, I looked up at him. He nodded, slowly pulled his cock out of my mouth. Tilting my head back and with the last full mouthful of piss, I gargled it, bubbles rising in the back of my throat, piss splashing the end of my nose. Happy with a hot man's urine in my mouth, happy with the grin spread across Ottavio's face, I swallowed the last of his piss with a satisfied gulp, and beamed.

"Eh, Papa Paolo," Ottavio said. "Tasty job."

"Papa Paolo?"

Ottavio chuckled, then his chuckle turned to laughter. He clutched his stomach, relaxed, laughing then plop! the buttplug fell onto the tiles with a splat, slick and glossy and black.

To be honest, the piss drink had done me in. I was sated. Full. Rooted. Could I have a raincheck on that second fuck?

Ottavio picked up the plug, licked it all over with his tongue, bent over as water showered his head and shoulders, and pushed it back inside his hole.

"Mate, I'm fucked," I said, standing up. "I don't have the cum to fuck you again."

Long-lashed pale blue eyes looked directly into mine. "But tomorrow? You fuck me tomorrow?"

"Sure," I brightened. "We can fuck tomorrow."

"Okay." Ottavio stuck out his hand. We shook on the deal. Warm water fell on our shoulders, and as I grabbed his foreskin and ran my wet finger inside it, around his cockhead, he slipped his tongue into my mouth and I tasted buttplug and arsejuice and cracksweat and my cum.

# A FUCKING BLESSING

One of my first impressions of Roma was of the sheer number of men walking about wearing cassocks: usually alone, concentration on their faces and in a hurry, like a fact-revealing cutaway in a European arthouse film.

Another was the charity calendars of handsome priests (fully clothed, damn!) – the calendario Romano – on sale in tourist shops and street stands. (Yeah, I bought one. December is the hottest, a true Christmas gift. But all those soulful eyes, generous smiles, inviting lips, some with cats …)

With more free time after the Giro d'Italia finished, I had a list of attractions to visit. (And I don't mean the men!)

Which is why I walked for 40 minutes, early one morning, to the Vatican.

I could've caught the Metro – all those crotches at eye-level when you're sitting on the bench seats; all those Italian men grabbing their cocks to adjust them every two minutes because that's what they're hardwired to do – but that would have meant walking from the Hotel Scenario in the opposite direction to … anyway, crotch-level-view be damned. I walked.

It was fucking early, but the sky was clear and bright and blue and I had booked on an 8.30 three-hour-tour of the Vatican Museums, Sistine Chapel and St. Peter's Basilica, maybe in that order. I was not wearing cycling shorts – yeah, the Vatican has a dress code – so I wore red casual shorts, tightly-cuffed at mid-thigh; and a white polo shirt, tight across my pecs, hem falling just below my belt (so when it rides up you can see my hairy stomach), sleeves cuffed at mid-bicep.

And a jockstrap. Sculpted, but understated. And the shorts (and the jock) show off my package and arse well.

I didn't take much note of the tour guide, a young dude with short dreads, dressed in a dark blue shirt with light cotton trousers. Reedy voice; pleasant, open face; but no revealing bulge nor taut biceps and chest. Slim. Or thin. Actually, rake thin. In need of sustenance. Maybe he should have demanded a pay rise or food vouchers.

It was crazy but the English-language tour of about 20 people moved swiftly (they have to, there are so many tours and tourists, even at 8.30am): gardens, rooms, courtyards, passageways, views, paintings, sculptures, tapestries, drawings, frescos, and more than a few men walking around in cassocks. Just darting through passageways and hallways, from building to building, looking busy. Heads down, avoiding glances. Or heads up, looking. When they're in a hurry, the summerweight fabric of their cassocks flutters behind them, the velocity sculpting their legs (and if you're lucky, their cocks) as they walk.

At one early stage, in yet another sculpture courtyard, I leaned against a pillar, kind of wanting the tour to end. Or move on. Or something. I was mulling over how to drill a hole in each of the three ten-cent coins deposited in my arsehole a few days earlier, to hang them on a chain, and how trying to organise a second fuck with Ottavio, the Ph.D student whose thesis on the US invasion of Sicily in 1943 had led to a cultural mix-up, had so far resulted in no seed being jointly spilled again.

Hot times. Waiting times. Frustrating times.

Walking through the courtyard, now also filled with milling tourists from other tours, I watched a man in a cassock dart from one closed-off passageway to another. Medium height, short dark hair, clean shaven, he cast a glance at the tourists as he shut the gate behind him, then tossed the quickest glance at me.

I craned my head to watch him disappear down the passageway. And as he turned right and placed his hand on a door handle, he glanced at me again. Stood for a split second or two or three or four

79

or five too long. Smiled. (Yeah, he smiled.) Then nodded, opened the door, and disappeared.

My spine straightened. Maybe my cock straightened a little, too.

But I'm not one of those blokes who lusts after men of the cloth. And it was just after 9.15am … isn't that too early to fuck?

We walked on. Two stolen sarcophagi (is that the plural?) and then another passage. Somehow the tour guides were guiding their groups through the maze of galleries without anyone stepping on anyone's toes (or official badges), but I saw my group a few metres or so ahead, short dreads way out in front, and wondered how I'd fallen behind.

And then I heard a creak off to the side and a door opened. A secret door. Secret in that it was a door, but part of the wall, and unless you knew it was there you wouldn't ever see it. A man in a cassock stood in the crack behind the open door, but the cassock was tenting in front, and in the light shining behind the door I could see a small wet patch at the front, too, like a damp pole held the tent up … or out. Looking at the man's artfully half-hidden face, he looked not unlike the man who had stood for a split second or two or three or four or five too long in the passageway off the sculpture courtyard.

Jaw ajar in wonder, I stepped towards him; the door opened further, I slipped through, and the secret door swiftly closed behind me. The priest, or brother (or what else is there?) turned and briskly, quietly headed up a small flight of stairs. Turning to hold his finger over his lips – shh! – I followed him around another corner down a dim hallway, then through an open doorway into a small office. The door clicked shut behind me. A key twisted in the lock.

White walls, a window overlooking another courtyard or garden (I couldn't tell) with deep red curtains, a desk and comfortable chair, filing cabinets, a tall, narrow cupboard, a large (oil?) painting on the wall and a cross: this was his office. At least for now.

I wasn't sure what I should do – genuflect? I looked at the man in the cassock – medium height, short dark hair, clean shaven, but now I had a better look: light hazel eyes, a piercing gaze, a thin smile stretched across even teeth, broad shoulders, a definite wet patch spreading across the front of his cassock. He stood with his back to the door, hands behind his back, holding onto the door handle.

Was I trapped?

Perhaps it was time for a charm offensive ...

I can talk to anyone. On any level. I'm no dummy.

Fucking a professor, I can use the kind of elevated and more complex language he'd speak in a faculty meeting. Fucking a tradie, I can fucking fuckin' use the swearing lingo he'd hear on a building site or sitting in the gutter at smoko. Fuck some dude and I can be jokey, man, and – well, get away with it.

But what language do you use with a priest?

I opened my mouth but he put his finger to his lips again – shh!

He crossed to the window and quickly drew the curtains. Then from a drawer in the desk, he pulled out a tube of lube and hitching his cassock over his hips, bent over the desk, exposing a fit arse with a light covering of dark fur. (Is freeballing a Vatican rule, too?) Looking at me from behind the desk, he pushed his arse out.

If he was inviting me for morning tea, I guess this was his way of serving it.

(And would the tour guide notice I was missing?)

I stepped behind the desk as he widened his feet. Watching his pink hole twitch, I pulled off my polo shirt, shucked off my red shorts, pulled down my jockstrap, and dropped to my knees. Interesting, as in the open desk drawer sat two metal cock cages. I pushed my tongue into his pinkness. He groaned, an instant inner release, and pushed his manhole back onto my face. It smelled fresh but masculine, and he grunted, reached back and grabbed the back of my head, grinding my face into his crack. I breathed in, not quite believing I was in the middle of Vatican City and had my tongue probing deep inside a priest's arse.

I ran my tongue around the edge of his hole, then nipped it with my teeth. He yelped, and shivered, then gathering his cassock bunched across the desk, he stood up, turned around, and lay on his back. You've done this before, mate, I thought, as he pushed his knees onto his chest and gave me better vantage at his fuckhole. He reached for the lube, handed it to me, then glanced at his watch.

"It's gonna have to be a quickie then, padre," I said.

I squelched a little lube on my cock – I like it sticky, not slippery – slicked it around the head and along the shaft, then poised it outside his trembling pucker.

Predictably (and I couldn't have asked for a better opener), he crossed himself – fingers touching forehead to mid-chest to left shoulder to right shoulder.

He breathed out, and I slowly inched my throbbing meat inside. He breathed in, slowly breathed out again, nodded, and as I gently pulled out and inched back in, he smiled, revealing straight teeth and relief.

No words – I guess the Big Fella doesn't know what's going on if he can't hear it.

And no touching either, hands rigid by his sides.

I focussed on my cock as it slid in and out of his hole. I could have snuck a look at the painting on the wall, but it might have been too confronting – in … and out … and in … and out – so I didn't.

But then I did, and it was abstract, awash with green and red – in … and out … and in … and out – and then looked down and saw him, cassock bunched up over his chest, looking at his watch again.

I shoved my cock deeper inside him. His ring sensed the urgency and clamped around my meat, as I fucked and fucked and fucked and fucked his hole.

He looked at me, mouth a wide 'O'. Hands immobile.

I picked up my rhythm, slamming into him as he lay on the desk. He whimpered with each thrust. Ech. Ech. I grabbed his balls and pulled them down towards my cock. Ech. His body spasmed. Stomach contracting, shoulders caving, he clenched as my cock ground into him. Throwing his head back, he gave a guttural cry. Hands still on the desk, his rock-hard cock shot a streak of cum across his stomach. He clutched at his cassock and pulled it up but just too late – a second ribbon of cum hit the middle of his chest, staining the

black fabric. And he kept cumming. And cumming, and cum ...
ming.

(I know that feeling, when you cum hands-free, no touching, you don't know what's fucking happening to your body but something inside you is bursting like, jeez ... nuclear fission, and your body just wracks forth and your balls churn over and your cock explodes and you're pumping pumping pumping jizz and you're covered and sticky and fucking wet and it's an amazing afuckingmazing feeling. Only had it happen to me twice, and I remember both times. And I want it again.)

"Miracolo," I said.

He smiled. And glanced at his watch.

I pulled out, and gripping my cock, pulled the skin back hard, tight, really hard, really tight, really really tight, so the skin on the head looked shiny and purple, like it was ready to burst.

"Time to get serious, padre," I whispered.

He craned his head to watch.

I enjoy an audience. I stroked with my free hand, rubbing along the incredibly taut, smooth shaft, grinding against it. I've been able to do this since my teens, pushing my glutes forward, skin straining against skin, breathing in, breath catching in my throat, pushing out further, harder, straining, stomach clenched and thighs clenched and cock clenched. And then a – a – a – a rush – and I shoved my cock back into his hole, spurting a rope of cum inside him. He groaned and eyes wide, bit his bottom lip, tilted his head back as I pumped deeper and pumped deeper and pump pump pumping flooded his hole with my hot sticky creamy ... exhausted ... fuckjuice.

Then stood.

Still.

Breathing.

Waiting.

Savouring the moment and my cock inside a man's contracting hole.

He smiled. Maybe because he had cum in his arse and a pool of cum swimming around his navel.

Pulling out of his hole, I leaned over and swirled his cum across the hair on his stomach with my tongue. He laughed – or giggled – so I leaned over further, cum sticking on my tongue, offering it to him. But he shook his head and wiped the leftover cum away with his cassock.

I swallowed, and wondered who does his washing.

He sat up to finish wiping himself off, then swung his legs over the side of the desk – in a very practiced way – and stood up. He opened the tall, narrow cupboard, pulled a coat (Vatican-issue?) off a coathanger and pulled it around his shoulders and chest, hiding the cumstreaks. He tossed me my polo shirt, closed the desk drawer with the lube back inside, and while I shrugged my shirt on, he snapped my jockstrap into place over my subsiding cock. I stepped into my shorts and he pulled them up and as I zipped up the fly and buckled my belt, he kissed me, on the lips, soft, tongue slipping into my mouth, just a little, a taste. A tongue taste. A tempting tongue taste.

Looking me up and down to check I was fully dressed, he opened the door. I followed him as he turned right and briskly, quietly headed down a dim hallway, left then right, and stopped at a narrow, beige door. Looking through a peephole, he turned to look at me again, slipped his hand into a pocket in his cassock and pulled out a business card, which he tucked into my shorts, touching my cock through the sheer pocket fabric. Glancing through the peephole again, he turned the door handle and pushed me through the narrowed doorway.

The door clicked oh-so-quietly shut behind me. It was a secret door. Secret in that it was a door, but part of the wall, and unless you knew it was there you wouldn't ever see it.

"This is the Gallery of Maps." The voice belonged to a young dude with short dreads, dressed in a dark blue shirt with light cotton trousers. He looked at me, nodded, and shared a lopsided smile. I stood behind the rest of the tour group, and cocked my head, to look like I was listening, suddenly interested. "The panels map the entirety of the Italian peninsula in large-scale frescoes," he continued, "and each depicts a region as well as a perspective view of its most prominent city."

I slipped my hand into my pocket and pulled out two things: the first was the card from the priest. *Piazza dei Quiriti, 4*, it said, with a mobile number, and *Rooms for Rent* above that, in English and next to that, presumably, the same in Italian.

The second was something I'd not realised the priest had also put there, as it certainly wasn't in my pocket earlier in the morning when I'd dressed. It was a ten-cent coin. I slipped it into my mouth, to see if it tasted much like the three ten-cent coins I'd earned a few days earlier in Vicolo delle Bollette.

I guess it did, though I couldn't quite remember. Pulling the coin from my mouth, I looked up as the tour group moved on, and into the eyes of the young dude tour guide with short dreads. He saw the business card and the ten-cent coin in my hands. And smirking, walked to the front of the group, said "This way please," and led them through another door.

# RIDING THE TOURIST TRAIL

I was stood up this morning, by a hot Brazilian I met at the Galleria Dell'Accademia.

So with one day left in Firenze – a town I expected to love, but don't – I sit on the upper deck of a hop on-hop off tourist bus charging around the city. Relax my shoulders, close my eyes.

And I had douched and all.

Grrr – no show, no go, no ho.

(And it's been seven days and no fuck!)

The red bus lopes up the hillside towards Fiesole.

I dip into my guidebook. 'Considered the most affluent suburb of Florence, with the highest median family income in the whole of Tuscany, Fiesole – '

I snap the book shut, face the breeze as the bus labours up the ascent, turns a hairpin, grinds up the next incline, churning along in low gear.

Breath catches in my throat. Looking east, the city stretches below along the Arno and after seven days, for the very first time, I see its real beauty, like 1950s Cinemascope: lush pastels beneath a lurid sky, terracotta rooves faded by the sun, trees gently sloping towards the city in the distance.

And I'm carping about a lost connection.

The bus pulls to a stop at the top of the hill, near Piazza Mino da Fiesole, the market square.

Grabbing my backpack, I scramble down the stairs to the lower level and step out onto the footpath. We've just missed lunch, and an ice cream parlour and a bar are both open, set with tables and chairs. There's an equestrian statue and official-looking vintage buildings and two other blokes stepping off the bus. One is tall, the other medium height; but both are solid, built, not an ounce of fat and all muscle, curvy with arms that cannot – will not – will never rest straight at their sides. Dedicated.

They're tourists like me: shorts and t-shirts, baseball caps and backpacks. Shaved heads.

They must be German: they're not wearing sunglasses. And I heard them speaking German earlier, standing in line, waiting.

They catch my eye and walk up the street, up the square, up, up ... off to the left ...

I walk in the opposite direction, past an official-looking building, down some stairs, along a path, smell olive from the olive trees and bay leaves from the bay laurels. (They're native to Fiesole: I read that in the guidebook.) Follow the path around the hill.

At a bend, I admire the view of Florence and the Arno and trees again. Slip off my backpack, pull out my water bottle, drink. Breathe out. It really is beautiful. So why do I feel I've wasted a week here?

"Hey."

Turning, I see the Germans sitting on a bench, just a little further up the slope. Admiring the view.

"We're admiring the view," the medium-height one says. With a British accent.

"Yes, it is an admirable view," says the taller one, who does have a German accent, but a slight one. Both watch me with startling blue eyes.

"You get the best view of Florence from up here," says the British-accented one.

"It is the best view," says the taller one. "Would you like your photo taken against this beautiful scenery?"

"Reinhard can take your picture if you like."

"I can take your picture. Kevin, you should stand in the photo, too," says Reinhard, standing up, all muscle man mountain. "Then I take the photo with you both."

"Do you mind if I stand in the photo with you, too?" Kevin asks.

They're like a vaudeville double act and I'm hearing them in Surroundsound.

Not thinking to disagree, I pull my phone out of my backpack. Kevin grabs it and passes it to Reinhard.

"I hope I don't look too tired," says Kevin, as Reinhard lines up the shot. "We still have entertaining to do."

"You do not look too tired, Schatz," says Reinhard. "You are too good-looking and too well-hung to look tired."

I look over my shoulder, position my feet so I'm not standing on a rock or a tree branch or a slippery slope, feeling slightly weird and pushed around. And wondering.

Kevin slips his massive left arm around me, hip bone against hip bone.

"Smile," says Reinhard. "It looks like you are making a new friend in this photo and having fun times."

Kevin's hand drops below my waist, and cups my left arse cheek.


"It's not far now," says Kevin, as he steps onto a steep narrow track.

"Yes, it is not far," adds Reinhard behind me.

"So you're an Aussie?" Kevin asks as we wend our way down the hillside.

"We are Ossies too," laughs Reinhard. "From Austria."

"Australians are everywhere in Italy," Kevin says.

Reinhard chimes in with something, but I'm not listening, as we approach a small clearing, lined with trees and what looks to be hidden from sight. Two used condoms lie on the ground.

"Ugh. These were not here this morning," says Reinhard, looking at Kevin. He picks up the condoms, sniffs them, puts them in his shorts pocket.

The men shuck off their backpacks, t-shirts, shorts and jockstraps, pile them beside a tree trunk. Their bodies are hairless, shaved, plucked. I'm not, so I wonder what they think as I shuck off my backpack, t-shirt, shorts and jocks, pile mine beside theirs by the tree, and stand in the middle of the clearing, clipped but still hairy: on my legs, my chest and stomach, a little on my back, my balls, and above my semi-erect cock.

"I love your fur," says Reinhard.

Kevin stands silent, long thick meaty cock proud and willing. (Reinhard was right, he IS well-hung.) His balls are tied with winding white cord, tied so they're separated, tight cord pushing them out and apart so they're hard and round and red and shiny and very very plump, like walnuts ready to be shelled. Sexy, and my cock shows its increasing appreciation.

"Yes, we love your fur," says Kevin, back in the moment. Bending over, he retrieves a tube of lube from his backpack.

With their sturdy bodies, their strength and physical presence, I feel a little overwhelmed with my narrower frame.

Reinhard's cock is also girthy and impressive – Kevin's is bigger – but he has the prize balls of the pair, tied up too, roped off and sectioned, ripe Victoria plums hovering in mid-air, ready for plucking and sucking, the white cord contrasting against his tanned boys. I want to eat them, drain their juice, roll my tongue around and bite and lick them.

Our cocks have all risen to the occasion, though my balls – not being tied up – are probably the only ones churning in their sack.

"Kevin needs to fuck arse," says Reinhard.

"And Reinhard needs to watch me fuck arse," says Kevin, slicking a little lube over his hard-on.

I assume I'll be fucked against a tree, but Reinhard sidles behind me, closes his arm around my chest, kisses my neck, pulls me against him. His cockhead nudges my lower back, his big bound balls push just above my crack. My cock is rock hard.

Reinhard wedges his hands under my armpits as Kevin steps in front of me. It feels like a set-up, as Reinhard hooks his elbows under my arms. Just as he lifts me off the ground, Kevin grabs my ankles. I'm suspended in mid-air.

"Put your legs on my shoulders," Kevin instructs, and his hefty shoulders slide under my calves so they rest either side of his neck. Knees bent, hips at right angles, my arse sits just above Kevin's thick tool, and with a grunt and a deft fondle, his meat stands poised just outside my pucker. I'm like a hammock strung between these two men.

Clearly, I won't be getting fucked up against a tree.

Kevin's cock slowly slides into my pucker. I'm used to the pleasure of long cocks but thick can be a challenge. Still, he's a skilled cocksman and as I relax my hole and lower my hips onto his pole he meets me halfway, sliding up inside my fucktube, smiling as he reaches the full depth of my arse.

"Feels good?" Kevin asks.

"In your arse?" asks Reinhard.

"Yes," I say, wondering how long they can keep up this human-hammock-fuck. Though as Kevin pulls out slowly and pushes back in, pulls out slowly and pushes back in, his arms wrapped around my legs as they're draped over his shoulders, Reinhard's grip under my arms is strong and resolute: he's clearly not going anywhere.

"Are you Kevin's cumdump?" Reinhard whispers just above my ear as Kevin's cock drills into me, each thrust an "ooph" as his bound knackers smack into my arse like ripe apricots thrown against a wall.

"You want his big daddy cock fucking your bitchcunt?" Reinhard coos as Kevin nails me. "You want his fuckmeat shooting his hot jizz deep inside your boipussy?"

Now, I am probably older than both these blokes, and I'm nobody's boy or boi or toy. Nor do I usually indulge in the feminisation of my genitalia, but sometimes you gotta go with the flow. So, "Fuck me, sir!" I say to Kevin, whose face is stone, a leer ground into his mug, blue eyes steel and grit and determination, jaw gnashing with each powerful thrust, eyes locked on mine as he owns my body and possesses my hole and SLAMS his meat into my guts.

"Fuck his boycunt!" Reinhard says. SLAM!

"Fuck me, sir!" SLAM!

"Fuck him!" SLAM!

"Fuck me!" SLAM!

"Fuck him!" SLAM!

"Fuck me!" SLAM!

And with each SLAM chimes the verbal "OOPH!" as his tight balls squash against my arse. OOPH! OOPH! OOPH!

"Slam your balls into him!" Reinhard says, and Kevin rams in deeper, faster – SLAM OOPH – SLAM OOPH – SLAM OOPH – SLAM OOPH –

Reinhard barks orders in German, but I am lost in the fuck, my head spinning as a breeze picks up, wafting through the clearing. Kevin's meat pistons into my fuckhole, my cock leaking seeping ooozing pre-cum onto my stomach hair as I hang between these two fuckmasters, Kevin ramming into my arse, bulk and muscle and meat excavating my hole and leaving no hormone, no nerve ending, no endorphin unturned, Reinhard holding me up with massive arms as they reduce me to a quivering mass.

Then Reinhard's grip under my arms slips. Kevin's face purples. His cock and his tight balls SLAM SLAM SLAM SLA-AAM into me. Then shucking my legs off his shoulders, his cock slides out of my hole. My feet hit the ground and Reinhard pushes me upright and off to the side. Kevin's grips his cock as Reinhard sinks to his knees in front of him, and with both hands reaches up and crushes Kevin's tight purple nuts – pushes them together and squashes them hard. "Eeeeerrrrgh!" Kevin screams but his shoulders hunch and his chest contracts and as Reinhard presses his balls tighter, grips them, clamps them, squeezes them like a fucking vice, Kevin jerk-jerks-jerks his cock, lets out a mighty HHHHOOWWWLLL and shoot-shoot-shoots ropes of white-hot sticky cum – gushes – sprogs – busts into Reinhard's waiting, open, willing mouth.

A breeze whispers through the trees.

Kevin powers down, bent forward, hunkered over his cock and Reinhard's shaved head, his crushed balls still held in the merciless grip of Reinhard's fists.

Reinhard's fingers slowly, slowly release their grip. He leans forward, and holding Kevin's cock up, licks, kisses Kevins's bound balls. Kevin shudders, his face shows pain, shows ecstasy, shows relief.

Reinhard stands, reaches over and arm pulls me into him, kisses me, opens my mouth with his tongue. He shares Kevin's big silky load with his probing, spreads the mancream across my lips, teases my tastebuds, slicks against my tonsils. Greedy, I suck it down, wanting to fill my gullet, sating my need for cum and connection and the taste of cock I've so far missed out. Reinhard reaches down and plays with my balls, too, his fingertips rough but light, pulling my sack, looping my knackers off like he wants to ringbark them.

"We like to share the load," Kevin says, as Reinhard licks my cheeks, my nose with his tongue, then kisses me on the lips and smiles.

Then, "Let me clean you up, Schatz," says Reinhard, and back on his knees again, he manhandles Kevin's balls as he licks the cum, the arsejuice, the sweat and the lube off his glistening, spent cock.

The bus pulls to a stop at the top of the hill, near Piazza Mino da Fiesole, the market square.

I wait to board as a tall guy in a faded orange t-shirt, lean and purposeful, steps off the bus. Like me, he's clearly a tourist: shorts and t-shirt, baseball cap and backpack. Can't be German as he's also wearing sunglasses.

His sense of purpose lapses as he catches my eye. Then looking to his right, spies the man mountains, neatly redressed, waiting …

Faded orange t-shirt walks off past an official-looking building, down some stairs, and out of sight.

Sliding into a seat on the upper deck, resting my backpack beside me, I pull out my guidebook. Then looking through the window, I crane to see the muscled backs of Reinhard and Kevin, walking up the street, up the square, up, up … and off to the left …

And I still haven't cum …

# FIRENZE FOURSOME

After my afternoon in the hills around Fiesole, I returned to my room on the third floor of the Grand Hotel Cavour for an extended nap. Then ventured out again after sunset, with backpack (sans cap) and the hope of a pleasant but restful final night in Firenze.

Florence is a town I had expected to love, but don't. Perhaps I visited the Galleria Dell'Accademia, and the Palazzo Pitti, and the Museo Dell'opera Del Duomo and the Uffizi too late in my stay, after the town's charm had worn its dull way with me.

And I am looking forward to catching the train back to Rome tomorrow. (Ah Roma, a city I had expected to dislike, but love … for all the reasons I thought I'd hate it!)

So standing on Via San Gallo, perusing the simple menu posted inside the glass-fronted display case, Ristorante Il Cardellino greatly appeals. I can sit at a small table by myself outside on the footpath, read my dog-eared copy of *Nights in Aruba*, and watch the world saunter by.

I am shown to the last table on the footpath by a gorgeous long-lashed, wide-shouldered, narrow waisted, pale faced but very smiley waiter. I order Spaghetti alla Vongole and Scaloppine al Limone "per favore" and a local beer and as I wait for the beer, open *Nights in Aruba*.

My copy has seen better days. It was bought in good condition from the secondhand Open Door Bookshop in Rome, but has been tossed between backpack and suitcase and train seats and hotel bedsides since. And I'm not making a lot of progress, either.

The older straight couple at the table beside mine push back their chairs and leave. The pale-faced waiter and another (perhaps his brother?) replace the tablecloth, reset new cutlery and glassware, and direct two new customers to their seats.

I flip to page 78 of *Nights in Aruba*.

My beer is placed before me and after a hefty glorious sip, I look up to see two men smiling.

"Hi."

"Hallo."

It's Kevin and Reinhard who are smiling. Kevin and Reinhard of the shaved heads and furious hammock-fuck with the squirrel-grip finish earlier this afternoon.

"It is good to see you again," says Reinhard, the taller man mountain.

Kevin the medium-height man mountain nods. His eyes look a little puffy.

I wonder if their balls are still bound tight with white cord, like they were when we fucked in the wooded clearing near Fiesole.

Words in Italian are exchanged with the pale waiter, who smiles – has he fluttered his long eyelashes at Reinhard? – and soon, Kevin and Reinhard are sitting at my table with their own beers. *Nights in Aruba* lies in front of me, bookmark protruding from pages 78 and 79, a reminder of hopefully returned to plans.

"My mother is English," says Kevin, "but my father is from Vienna."

"My family is from Wien," says Reinhard.

"And we live in Vienna together and have for ten years."

"Yes, we have been living for ten years together in Wien."

I sip my beer again, and nearly choke when Kevin says, a little louder than I would have expected, "And we owe you an orgasm."

The waiter, two tables over, stops his pouring of wine into a glass. When he resumes, a smirk creeps across his face.

Our food arrives. I order and drink two more beers – it's hot, and the waiter is very obliging and extra-smiley – so really, when our meals are finished and the waiter clears the plates and serves the digestivi – I think I have limoncello, of course … I think that's what I order (or have ordered for me) ... whatever I drink, it's smooth, velvety, lemony, not tart, not sweet.

But I am a bit of a two-pot screamer.

Reinhard and Kevin are friendly all evening, joking and smiling and both fondling my legs and up into my crotch under the table (though at different times) and I don't pull away (there is no room, really, to retract either leg or my crotch without moving tables or leaving Ristorante Il Cardellino completely) and then Reinhard says something in Italian again, to the waiter, and the waiter checks his wristwatch and replies in Italian and then we wait some more and Reinhard and Kevin order another beer each (I decline as I need to get my head back together again) and they drink their beers and then the waiter stands by the restaurant door smoking as the restaurant appears to be closing as all the other outside tables are stacked inside and Kevin says "You coming?" and Reinhard says "Come on" and Reinhard says something in Italian to the waiter who says "Sì" and I shove *Nights in Aruba* in my backpack and sling it over my shoulder and we walk to the Hotel Spadai which is opposite the Duomo and we ride the lift up to their suite and then ...

I wake up a while later, lying on my back – fully clothed – spread across a large bed. Did that limoncello work wonders? Dunno, but as a completely naked hairless Reinhard (ha! not even his balls are tied) passes me a large glass of water and standing up, I drink it all down, some of it spilling down my chin and neck and onto my t-shirt. He growls in approval and tweaks my nipples. He takes the empty glass from me, and I turn to see a rutting couple on a bed in the next room. Fuck it's hot. Kevin's Topping the waiter, behind and above him, so bulldog, which – fuck! it's my favourite position after being enveloped in missionary – just turns me on so much. My cock hardens in my shorts as I watch Kevin's meat drilling into the waiter's hairy hole, but I also see, his hips open wide for the best driving angle, Kevin's tanned and shaved pucker. Two tight, giving puckers for the price of one. Few sights are better than that!

I'd love to push something through Kevin's sphincter. My mouth salivates at the sight, the thought, the sensation of my tongue deep within the folds of his manhole. Kevin's cock piledrives into the waiter's arse, who greets each thrust with a grunt.

Kevin's balls swing freely too, no tied-up tension in those boys.

"Kevin is a major fucker. I love to watch him fuck arse," says Reinhard.

I look down and see Reinhard stroking his meat. I am torn – I want to watch Kevin's expert pistoning, the grim set of his chin and the ecstacy on the waiter's face as Kevin fucks the shit out of him, maybe even fill his mouth with my own cock – but Reinhard's impressive fuckstick, wet with pre-cum, meaty under his caress, ever ready for penetration, is millimetres from my hands, only centimetres from my arse and just a little further from my mouth.

"I am on a mission for your orgasm," says Reinhard, suspiciously robotic. Then he laughs and grabs my hard-on through my shorts.

"And my plums are free tonight," he adds, reaching down and giving his hangers a tug.

I fall back onto the bed and in seconds my clothes are piled on the floor. As the grunts from the next room grow deeper and louder and stronger, Reinhard goes to work on my balls, sucking them, licking them, kissing them, rolling them around his mouth and holding them, feeling their weight. Then quickly they're encased in something … I sit up on my elbows and look down, see he's wrapped a silicon ball stretcher around my boys, which feels soft and welcoming on my ballsack. And my nuts hang low under the stretcher.

Reinhard kneels at the end of the bed, his cock so hard it strains taut within its skin. "Jerk your cock," he says.

My mind is too mellow and my body too relaxed to do anything else, so I oblige. Pull my meat, jerk it slow so my balls thwack under the ball stretcher, bounce with each stroke.

Reinhard's gaze focuses on my nuts, fingers itching to stretch my ballsack, pull it down, grip the skin so my boys pop out of their bag.

And I'm jerking but the pounding drilling filling coming from the other room is distracting and I wonder if I even have enough in me to cum.

"I help you," Reinhard says. Placing his hand between my legs, he taps my balls.

Just a little. A light smack, with his fingers.

I start, breathe in. Let out a skewed sigh.

His fingers tap my balls again, a little harder.

"Ah," I gasp.

"You like it?" asks Reinhard.

"Yes," I surprise myself.

"Keep jerking," he says, and taps my balls a little harder again, so my boys feel pain, but above them too, just above the line of my trimmed pubes, just under my stomach.

"Again," I say.

Tap. The pain is dull but real and I want more.

"Again."

Tap.

"Harder."

Reinhard swings into it, tapping harder, a light smack.

My cock is wet with pre-cum and I grind my cock. "More."

Harder. I want to really feel it.

Reinhard grabs my balls and ringbarking them with his thumb and index finger, pulls them down so they're taut and firm and can't move. Then smacks them.

"Aaw!" I groan, the pain rising up to my stomach.

"Again?"

"Yes!"

SMACK!

Fuck! the pain is instant, rising into my guts but it's so there! as my pelvis tilts to dull the shock.

SMACK!

"Reinhard – "

But he answers with more tapping on my balls, low and constant and rhythmic, not the shock of the smacks but I know I'm fucking alive with each tap, each jolt up my balls.

Reinhard grins, like he's revealed the secret to eternal life and he wants to share it.

"There is no going back now," he says, shaking his head.

I'm rubbing and jerking and grinding my cock but it's my knackers I'm really connected to. I have always loved having them pulled down, stretched, held tight, licked and sucked and rolled around a hot wet willing mouth, but this is next level, painful but oh so fucking pleasurable too, hitting me right where I live.

Orgasmic moans sound from the other room. I turn to catch Kevin ramming deep inside the waiter's hole, cock pulling out of the waiter's hairy open expectant pucker, then slammed back in to the waiter's grunts and Kevin's extended groan.

Reinhard ups the tempo, and he's slapping my balls now, counting each moment of hard contact – "68, 69, 70."

I gasp and feel the pain in my balls and the ache in my gut and the tingle on my ballsack but the slapping won't quit and I don't want it to and I wheeze a low cry and drop my pelvis – "87, 88, 89" – then Kevin's kneeling beside me on the bed, sticking his wet cummy cock in my open mouth and the waiter looking pale and sated and truly fucked leans over and squeezes my nipples "96, 97, 98" and I grind low, deep and "99" SMACK! my balls lurch upward and I cum I fucking cum grind cum shoot cum wads of milky roping sprogging white fucking hot jizz across up over beyond my stomach, pumping – tap – breathing – "101" – smiling – "102" – shuddering ... giggling ... laughing – yeah – a gentle "103" – cumming always makes me laugh.

Then cry out as Reinhard licks my balls, pulls the ball stretcher off me, slides his fingers around my knackers and gives them a rough final jerk.

I lean up on my elbows, shake my head at Reinhard, my legs spread, tingling balls hanging low over my arsehole. "Yes, there is no going back now," I say. Then lick my lips, tasting Kevin's cum and the waiter's arsejuice on my lips.


The elevator doors open and the waiter and I, backpacks slung across our shoulders, step inside. We're waving good night goodbye bon voyage to Kevin and Reinhard, both standing in bathrobes in the hallway.

And as the elevator chimes, Kevin's eyes widen, he looks at me earnestly and asks, "What's your name?"

But the doors close. And as the elevator begins its descent, the waiter, pale and exhausted but with intense eyes behind exquisitely long lashes, says, in perfect Italian-accented English, "Signore, I did not cum."

# SÌ BELLO, ARRIVEDERCI

I wish I loved Firenze, but I don't.

The city is beautiful, but you can't walk, eat or yawn for all the tourists: they are every-fucking-where! I feel guilty for not liking Florence yet also guilty for being part of the problem!

So when Matteo the waiter from the restaurant, lift descending from our foursome with Kevin and Reinhard the muscle mountains from Vienna, said in perfect Italian-accented English, "Signore, I did not cum," my heart lurched.

Neither could I say no to his eyes, intense behind such exquisite lashes as they begged me to help him get off.

But he won't go back to my room at the Grand Hotel Cavour: he has a cousin who works there as a night porter. When I suggest going back to his place, his shoulders shrug, he mutters something in Italian and blanches even paler in the streetlight.

So we catch a tram (our legs touch as we ride) and after three stops find ourselves in the large Parco delle Cascine. Where you can also catch glimpses of the Arno if you try. (Though not much can be seen in the dark!)

People mill around and not every man is here for sex (probably all tourists!) but as I follow Matteo's wide shoulders and white shirt and narrow waist, he turns and smiles, checking I am still here, face angelic in the moonlight, his exceptionally long lashes casting shadows across his wan cheeks.

But I've seen his cock (when it was flaccid) and it's worth waiting for.

He walks faster than I do, so I hurry to keep up, my backpack (and the damn copy of *Nights in Aruba*) slapping against my back.

It's cooler in the park, a breeze blowing from the hills nearby, and despite my tiredness (I keep yawning) and Matteo's haste (he keeps looking over his shoulder at me) the brisk walk is not unpleasant.

Matteo steps off a path and heads across a large patch of unmown grass toward a clump of trees, beckons me. "Sì," I say and follow his footsteps, grass crunching flat under our feet. My pupils widen as we enter the thicket, and putting my hand in my pocket, I feel my cock hardening in my jocks. I had not expected even one session today, my final day in Florence, let alone three.

The thicket is dark, despite moonlight above, and I see distant figures, doing what I can't be sure until my eyes adjust.

Matteo stops under a large tree, a canopy of foliage to half-hide us. As I close in his hands slip around my waist, then pull my backpack off my shoulder, deftly drop it on the grass. Then he grabs my t-shirt, clasps me tight, pushes my lips open with his tongue. I smell cigarette smoke (in his hair? his white shirt? on his skin?) but taste alcohol. Did he have a beer at Kevin and Reinhard's, or did he drink on the job? His hard-on throbs through his thin trousers as he presses into me. His tongue darts across my tongue, sucks it down, lashes across my teeth, and I lose myself in his ardent kisses, hard and hungry and hopeful.

He unbuckles his belt, trousers falling to the ground. My shorts and jocks do the same. I step out of them for easier access and then throw my t-shirt on the pile beside my backpack.

Our hard cocks meet mid-air and he grabs them both, holds them, squeezes them together, a cock sandwich, jerks them both, rough and ready. He steps out of his trousers, turns around and bends over, outstretched hands holding himself away from the tree. He pulls his shirt up and reveals his arse, white in the moonlight but toned and taut, reaches under his balls and sticks a finger in his hole, fucks himself a little, inviting me to sample his pucker.

I squat down and stick my tongue inside. He quivers, shivers, growls low and whispers something in Italian. His arse is hairy, and I slowly taste his hole, my tongue light on the skinfolds, deeper in the centre, pulling it apart as I search for pleasure, the meaning of life, his soul. A good rim job can feel like the Top is reaching into the very depths of your being, and I want to open him up so I feel his beating heart and enter his mind and fill all his senses with ache and pleasure and longing. And what I taste is leftover mansweat and Topcum and fuckjuice from the pounding he took earlier from Kevin.

"Fuck me, signore," he whispers. "Fuck me now."

I stand, press my cockhead against his pucker. His hole is moist and open and I slide my meat inside him. It's sticky, not juiced up with lube, so more friction, more skin-on-skin, more heat.

Pushing into him, he rocks against the tree, whimpers as he feels every millimetre of my cock sliding deep into him, whimpers as I slowly pull out, out of his pucker so it cools in the night air and then sighs as I slide into him again. I slap him on his arse, lightly to gauge his reaction.

"Sì, sì, sì, bello, bello, bello," he whispers, head shaking with pleasure, with pain, who knows, but his fucktube fits snug around my cock. And my balls, still sore from Reinhard mangling them, buffet with pleasure and pain and more pleasure against Matteo's arse with each probing entry.

Matteo tightens his ring, and I groan with the extra friction. My cock, muscular and veiny, made to measure, looks fucking amazing sliding inside his pale arse. A young fit fella approaches, dark-haired with an eight o'clock shadow, t-shirt slung over one shoulder and shorts slung over the other, dark hair on his chest and stomach. He stands pulling his hard-on and watching us fuck, cock and arse, pole and hole, meat and gape. He reaches over and pulls on my nipples, then kisses me long and deep, tongue fucks my mouth as my cock fucks Matteo's arse.

He growls, hand grips my arse, pushing me deeper into Matteo's hole. Then he stands behind me, his hard cock under my arse and wet cockhead pressing into my balls, frotting between my thighs, fingers reaching around and grinding my nipples.

He's putting me off my game, and as I sink against him, head lolling as I look up at the starry sky, Matteo slides off my cock, drops forward, stands up. Angry words are exchanged (in Italian) between him and the naked dude behind me, who withdraws his cock from between my thighs.

Matteo grabs me, pushes me against the tree. He shoves his hand up under my arse, probing for my hole. More angry words spit between Matteo and the dude, who backs away, arms bent up at the elbows, shoulders raised in questioning surrender.

Matteo pushes my head down, and I hear the squirty sound of lube and then Matteo's long thin cock (I take long cocks like a champ) poises just outside my pucker, slides in, no resistance, just like it is meant to at night in a large park in Florence in summertime when men are horny and need hot anon cock-and-cum contact.

Matteo fucks me, pushes my head against the tree, the bark rough on my face. He whispers to the dude, who crouches down, peering up, watching Matteo's cock saw into my hole. I push my hole out, craving more cock, face grinding against the bark as Matteo shoves my head down, taking control of the fuck, of me, of the whole fucking night. Working up a rhythm to his familiar grunts, the traction between fuckstick and fuckhole crackling, my back slicks with sweat. His fingers dig into my hips, pull me back onto his cock as it powerdrives into me.

Grabbing my throat, Matteo jerks my head back. I gasp as he thrusts deep deeper deepest into me, my legs aquiver, breathing shallow. Then I feel a tug, a hold, a grip on my nuts. The naked dude has them in his grasp, pulling them. More words from Matteo, and the dude rings my balls tight tighter tightest and with his other hand, whacks them. HARD.

I almost jump out of my skin, but Matteo has hold of my hips, cock impaling me as WHACK! my boys are smacked again. They sting, writhe in agony in my ballsack, but fuck! so much pain, so much eye-rolling pleasure! I groan up at the sky. Matteo whimpers and my hole feels the first cum pump. My sphincter twinges, grips his meat as his balls shoot into me, hot jizzy cum ... shoot ... sprog ... pump ... empty ... drain ... drip ... trickle ... cum ...

My hole relaxes, opens wider, wants more hot cum more more more. Flooded with cum, I know it's flooded with cum and my hole knows it's flooded with cum but still, we want more!

Matteo staggers back, and a rush of cool air flushes my spent gape. The dude grabs my arse, pulls me towards him, sticks his tongue in my hole and eats me, licks me deep inside, sucks my hole, slurps it so I hear sproggy slops guzzling down his throat. He won't quit, gnawing at my arse, desperate for every last lingering lap of Matteo cum.

Matteo pulls him off me. I watch him kiss the dude, share the load, run the sticky residue across his face with his tongue, hold him at the back of the neck so he can't get away. Then Matteo caresses his face with soft, loving fingertips. The dude sniffs, and if I'm not mistaken, in the moonlight, a tear courses down his cheek.


Walking back to my room at the Grand Hotel Cavour (last tram was over an hour ago), my backpack on my back, the infernal copy of *Nights in Aruba* lolls inside. My balls ache and my arse gapes raw. My throat, parched, needs a massive drink. But I can't help but smile. It may look like a grimace to an observer but still, I am smiling.

I'm not sure if I shot my load. Maybe it was a half-sprog. My cock is wet and sticky in my jocks, so when I was being fucked deep and my balls were having the shit whacked out of them … dunno.

Would I come back to Florence? That is not in my plans. But the last 12 hours or so go some way to tipping the scales in favour of a return visit …

# LADS

# TOOLING THE TENNIS CHAMP

'Hot pic in your bike shorts,' the message read.

I'm wearing white cycling shorts in the photo. And what you see most – I'm leaning back against my bike, feet crossed in front: I was in Rome for the Giro d'Italia – are my knackers, gloriously front and centre, round and full and brimming with pride and potency.

So we swapped photos, swapped messages, swapped fantasies, swapped mobile numbers. And he's a hot-looking guy – clear olive skin; short, dark hair with a coif; tall, lean sportsman's build. A handsome dude who'd pique any man-on-man interest.

But … Jesús is 19. And I don't really do twinks. I mean, I do do twinks. But I don't do twinks with "daddy" issues. Total turn-off.

After I chain my bike to a pole on the footpath outside his house, 'Come round the back,' he texts, 'I'm in the shed.'

I saunter round the side of the house, adjusting my cock in my navy blue shorts (the white cycling shorts are in the wash) and hope that whatever's in the shed, it's hot and heavy and needs a hand.

I spy the shed across the back lawn. The door is open.

Poking my head inside, I see a tall, fit, olive-skinned athlete wearing a white tank top and short short white shorts. Holding a tennis racquet in his hand.

"Hey, bro," he says, dropping the racquet on a leather sofa.

Bro? At least it's not "Hey, daddy."

"Hey, Jesús."

Jesús flashes me a broad smile: white teeth and a sexy grin. "You said my name correctly," he says. "You speak Spanish?" A light moustache lines his upper lip.

He closes the shed door and latches it shut. Then slipping his arms around my back and gripping my arse with both hands, draws me into him.

"No, I've just had some practice at curling my tongue around Spanish names," I say.

I like his tall, lean, defined body. I like his hot, funky summer-heat smell. And I like his confident cock, already straining in his short shorts as he grinds into my package.

"My parents are in Colombia for two months," he says, tongue twisting around 'Colombia' like a native. "But I'm staying here because I have to play in some tournaments."

The shed has been fitted out like a clubhouse. Plasterboard lines the walls, carpet covers the floor. Shields and trophies and cups and platters are displayed in cabinets. And mounted in the centre along the back wall is a large photo of Jesús, looking hot and sweaty in tennis gear, holding a gold medal on a blue ribbon.

Taking the lead, Jesús pushes me down onto the sofa, then straddles my legs, his arse grinding into my thighs, his chest rubbing against my pecs. He opens my mouth with his tongue, probing past my lips, huffing down my manscent as he sinks deep into kissing me, fingers gripping my nipples.

My hands run down his back, squeeze his arse. Fingers slide inside the waistband of his shorts.

He pulls away, shucks off his tank top over his head. "I earn money from playing tennis," he says. "But I also recycle old racquets."

Okay, I nod, wondering: where is this headed?

"Usually for money."

Jesús slips off my lap and picks the racquet up off the sofa. Twirling it in his hand, it looks a little old and worn and used but treasured.

His cock bounces as his shorts drop to the floor – he's going commando – then stepping out of them, he picks up a tube of lube lying beside the sofa. Holding the racquet upside down, rounded top of the racquet head touching the carpet, he glops lube on the end of the handle.

I nod again, watching.

Naked, hard veiny cock standing to attention in mid-air, cockhead already covered in leaky pre-cum, Jesús smooths lube down the grip of the handle with two fingers. The grip has been worn smooth but from what – a lot of playing, or a lot of playing?

"And sometimes I keep them and use them for fun," he adds, tossing the lube on the floor.

Leaning forward, he reaches behind his arse and positions the racquet handle just outside his hole. And then he slowly … slowly … nudges backward … eases downward; closes his eyes and winces as his arsehole oh-oh-opens up to push oh-oh-over the handle lip and down-down over the shaft; slowly. Slowly. Slooow-ly …

When he breathes out half of the racquet handle has disappeared inside his arse. He wriggles his hole around the handle.

Am I really needed here?

"Thank God for gravity," he says. And then he tilts his pelvis forward, just a little, and lowers his hips, down further, taking the racquet handle deeper, deeper again, burying it inside his fuckhole. Opens his mouth as a long breath escapes. Opens his eyes; looks beckoning at me.

I could ruminate about the arrogance of youth and the assumption that his charm and energy and beauty will make me do as he wants.

But I step over to him anyway. The racquet handle wedged in his arse, he pulls down my shorts. My cock is hard and leaking inside my jock. He pulls down my jock, grips my balls, pulls my balls down long and hard. I moan. The racquet head lodged against the carpet, he rides up and down on the racquet handle, each bounce pulling on my ballsack. I spread my feet and open my stance so he can get a bigger, tighter grip.

"These are what I really wanted," Jesús says, jerking them harder. "They look so good in your bike shorts in that photo."

"Yeah," I gasp, as he rides and tugs, bounces and pulls, writhes and squeezes. "When they're peaking, they're a fucking handful."

"Pinch my nipples," he says. So I lick two fingertips and lightly – barely – caress his nipples.

He slides down the racquet handle again, bouncing at the bottom then cresting at the top.

"Harder," he demands. "More."

I grab his nipples and pinch them harder, pincer them between my fingernails and pull them out from his chest.

As he rides up and down, I pull his nipples and he yanks on my balls, a fucking turbine of pheromones and hormones and secretions and heat. He strokes his cock a little, but not seriously. 'Cause the main action is the racquet handle ratcheting inside his arsehole.

He grunts, a guttural groan from the depths of his guts.

Sweat pours down my face, stinging my eyes. I close them –

Jesús grabs my attention by yanking extra hard on my balls, scraping them down with such tight force I imagine they're going to pop out of the bottom of my ballsack and roll onto the floor.

My eyes flash open again, though they still sting, and watch as he slides halfway, more than halfway up the handle, then slams his arse down hard on the throat of the racquet. Rises up, then slams down hard. Pistons up then pounds down hard. His mouth widens as his arse works the racquet … or the racquet works his arse … slam! – and slam! – and slam! – and slam!

My balls are aching under his grip, and I latch onto his nips again and pull and yank and yank and pull –

And then he pistons up … halfway, two-thirds, three-quarters up the shaft … and then he tilts forward and makes little jerks, moaning, the handle end not so far inside his fuckhole now, just … … …

Then he growls, as the handle tip rubs … presses down … pressing … pressing … gasping and … catching his breath … buffing … rubbing … his prostate.

His lips open, breath rasping in. His eyes glaze over, roll back in their sockets –

His cock spasms, and gripping my balls tighter, squeezing them as he pulls them down 'til they're stretched to their hot, achingly painful exploding limit, I mooooan just as he cries out. I push his erect nipples in hard hard HARD with my fingers just as he nuts – nuts warm thick cum – nuts jets of warm creamy cum – ropes of hot sticky manjuice – thick sticky creamy hot funky cockmilk – over and across and down my quivering thigh.

Ah, the wonder of youth – assuming I want his hot creamy cum sliding in thick streaming streaks down my leg.

(But I do!)

Jesús slides back down on the racquet handle, breathing out long and low. His hand releases the vice on my balls and wasting no time, knackers tender and banging against my thigh, I scrape his dripping cum off my leg with my fingers. Scooping his manjuice up with my hands. Sticking cummy fingers in my mouth. Swallowing his jizz like it's a fucking protein shake and I'm a supplement junkie.

There's so much cum, a river of it, still sticky on my leg and wet on my hand, he can't have nutted for –

"I haven't cum for two days," Jesús says, laughing.

Ah, the joys of youth! His cup runneth over … and I want all that sprog down my throat.

"But I can go again in fifteen minutes if you want," he adds.

He reaches behind him and contracting his stomach muscles, pushes the tennis racquet out of his arse. Looking me in the eyes and smiling – I'm still licking his cum off my fingers – he opens his mouth and runs his tongue along the wet shaft.

Then hands the racquet to me and says, "You're turn now."

I take it, twirl it in my hand, his arsejuice and spit spreading across my palm.

Then I grab the tube of lube off the floor, glop just a few drops on the handle (not too sloppy, 'cause I like a bit of friction), and grease it up ready for the next game.

Because that's what a good sport does.

# SHOWER SCENE

I've had a gutful.

That's four loads down my throat (and now deep inside my gullet), and three more in my arse, keeping it nicely lubed and ready for the fourth or fifth or sixth or seventh load, should my hole start twitching for some more attention.

But it's Friday night (or Saturday morning) at the sauna and at 1.30, my holes need a break.

So, with seven cumloads rolling around inside me and a smile plastered at both ends, I head downstairs to the showers.

The showers are empty as I hang my towel on a hook. Choosing the shower at the far end, I turn the tap and stand under the jet of warm water, dipping my head as it flows across my shoulders, down my back, over my chest, off my sore and tender nipples.

Looking out under the curtain of spray, I see I've been joined in the next shower by a hot twink. He turns and smiles, bending to soap up his legs as the water hits his shoulders, turning a little so I can see the curve of his arse.

I'm not much into twinks. But I recognise a hot guy when he's waving his arse at me. And he's tall and nicely built – not lean, not monster-muscled, but curvy – clear, pale skin, high cheekbones and a dark crewcut. He soaps his biceps, then flops his cock out with his hand and cups his balls as he washes them, water jetting off the end of his cockhead.

Mmmm ... I don't know what it is about running water, but just the sound of the showers and the look of the twink and the sly glances he's giving me ... I can feel the piss backing up in my bladder, above and behind my cock and balls.

I look at the sign stuck on the wall above the tiles – 'No Sex in Shower Area'.

And suddenly, despite feeling kind of full – with cum, with piss, with the fuzz of a heady night at the tubs – I'm still looking for something more.

The twink turns towards the wall and throws his head back. Water splashes off his pecs. I chuckle to myself – it's like a TV ad for cologne, him shaking his head (like a dog! Though there's not a lot of hair there with his crewcut!) and me (almost) drooling, wanting to catch his eye again.

But I need to piss before I do anything else. Before my cock hardens perving at the cute twink. So I grab my cock and directing it down towards the drain running along the back of the showers, shoot a short jet of piss.

I glance over at the twink and see he's watching my cock. So I direct it towards the drain again, but just a little further over this time, a little closer to his feet, another short piss spurt.

He steps closer, soapy lather in his hand, rubbing across the top of his very short pubes. He looks in my eyes and smiles, then sticks out his tongue and licks his bottom lip, slowly, slightly, just so I can see.

I shoot a longer, harder, heavier piss stream, but just miss the drain this time, splash his feet a little.

His rubbing across the top of his pubes slows.

So I release the full stream. My piss washes his feet. I direct the stream up his legs and he turns around, piss hitting his muscled calves. The full feeling above and behind my cock and balls is emptying. I know the sign says 'No Sex in Shower Area' but this isn't sex really, is it? It's just two fellas pissing about and having fun.

He steps closer again and I feel warm piss sprinkle on my skin as it splashes off his legs and onto mine. He cups his hand under the stream and piss pools in his palm. Will he drink it? Flick it back onto me? But he tips it over his cock, grinning like he's found a new toy and he's unsure if he should be playing with it but it feels so good and …

My piss trickles to a stop.

His fingertip touches the end of my cock, smears the last drip of piss across the piss slit. "You got any more?" he asks.

"Nah, mate," I say. "I'm all out now."

I shrug my shoulders. He stares at my cock.

"You got any in you?" I ask.

"Yeah," he nods. He looks over his shoulder. No audience. No sauna staff. "I've never done this before," he adds under his breath.

"Cool you've got some in you," I say. "And it's always good to share."

I touch the end of his cock with my fingertip, encouraging it like my finger's a water diviner. Then I crouch down in front of his cock, the flow from the shower spilling over my head and shoulders and down my back.

He squares his hips toward me. If I tilt my head I can see behind him, looking out for sauna staff.

He leans closer to me. I grab him by his hips. And open my mouth.

And sit back, on my haunches, waiting for that sweet yellow stream.

He sighs, closes his eyes, relaxes his shoulders, leans back so his cock pushes forward.

Performance anxiety is a real thing. Some guys just can't piss in front of other guys, no matter how full their bladder, how much they've drunk in the last two hours, how great their desire to let flow with a full stream of golden spray.

He rocks back and forth, just a little …

I breathe out, lick the tip of his cock.

He shudders … and then it happens. At first a trickle across my chest … then a stronger flow onto my chin … and then a full heavenly piss stream across my lips and into my open mouth.

I'm greedy when it comes to piss. As a full-on piss-pig, the big question is always: just where do I direct the piss? I don't want to miss a salty drop, so do I swallow it all, sucking it down into my gullet ... or let it flow over my face and chin and neck and nipples and wallow in it, scrape it up with my fingers and lick them dry or ...

Nah, I'm a chug-it-all-down kind of guy! So pulling his hips closer, I lock my lips around his cockhead, and feel the warm piss flow over my tongue, pulsating down my throat, cascading into my guts. It's like I'm meant to do this, in the showers at the sauna, savouring the twink's warm natural juices, collecting his essential resources, showing young guys the pleasure they can take in their own bodies and the bodies of other men.

And my cock is rock hard, bouncing between my legs with each sucking swallow.

I drink it all down. Every warm musky sulphury drop. Glug glug glug. Sharing a manly bond with a hot twink over nature's goodness. To drink a man's entire load of piss, you need incredible trust and real intimacy.

I look up at his face as he looks down on me, smiling, grinning, shaking his head with pleasure, happy to find release in my mouth.

And I don't want this chugfest to end.

But it does ...

"Hey, fellas," a gruff voice says.

The twink turns around, the last drops of piss spraying across my face and onto the wall. I'm still crouching on the floor, shower water falling on my back and shoulders.

A muscled sauna staffer stands at the end of the showers, shaking his head. "Not here, fellas," he says.

The twink grabs his towel and as he wraps it around his waist, "Thanks, champ," I say.

The twink disappears.

I stand and wipe my mouth with the back of my hand. The sauna staffer looks at me with his steely blue eyes, and I take in the dark stubble on his chin, the erect nipples through his muscle tee. As he stands in front of me, he pulls at his crotch through his tight shorts.

"I'm knocking off in five minutes if you want more of what you've been drinking," he says in my ear.

I nod.

"And I've been saving it up all night." He grins, tweaks my nipple, pulls it down hard, presses it back into my chest.

I swallow the nipple pain. My cock is hard again, bouncing between my thighs.

"Meet me in the smokers' courtyard," he says. "Ther're a few fellas out there already who might want to help quench your thirst."

He sticks his finger inside my mouth and I clamp my lips around it. "And sharing is caring," he adds.

He reaches down and grips my balls in a tight squeeze. "Five minutes," he adds, then giving my ballsack an extra tug, he grabs my towel off the hook, throws it at me, and walks out.

# DREAM IT, THEN CREAM IT

"Paul?"

I blink. Not from the midday sun, but because I am not used to hearing him say my name.

He stands outside Henryk's front door. I am dog-and-housesitting while Henryk is in New Zealand for two weeks. (Dunno why he's in New Zealand. I didn't ask.)

My mouth twists from a surprised 'O' to a more welcoming smile. "Gael."

"Henryk isn't here?" Gael asks.

Twice a year, I teach a two-nights-a-week, four-week-long adult education course about small business, usually called 'Working from Home in Your Own Business: What to Do and What Not to Do'. (The name of the course is longer than the course itself!)

Many in my class are recent migrants or international students.

Just last week, on the last night of the course, Gael spent a long time gathering his books, his pens, his computer, and his courage. I thought he might ask for a higher mark on his final assignment. (He was capable of earning a higher grade but had not put in enough effort.) But as I nipped around the classroom flicking off lights, he asked with a laugh, "Teacher, do all men in Australia want open relationships?"

By his laughter, I knew his question was genuine.

"I don't know," I said.

"All the men I meet on apps want an open relationship. I met this guy, two guys ..."

I sat on the edge of a student desk, swung my legs under me to keep the mood light. "Men aren't usually on apps looking for relationships."

"How can I meet the men who are looking for relationships?"

I don't think I gave him a proper answer.

So here he is now on Henryk's (and my temporary) front doorstep. 27 years old (so half my age: I remember from his enrolment info), medium height, short dark hair and olive skin, a light moustache and wide goatee, brown eyes. Handsome but not drop-dead-Hispanic-gorgeous, so approachable. Dressed in a loose tank top, with a sparse tattoo creeping up his upper arm and across his shoulder, and sporty shorts, though I know he is not in the least sporty. Plus, he's from Mexico, where some of my sweetest, nicest, most genuine students come from.

"I saw you online," he says, with his slight and beguiling accent. "Dick Cavern?"

Oh my God, he knows about my one-shot porn career! Although (and I feel my balls roll and my cock rise a little in my jocks) there are worse things a hot young Mexican dude could know about me.

"I have been reading your hot stories, too."

Okay, so he knows that, too. I write stories about my (sex) life and they are published online. Maybe Henryk told him about the porn and the stories, which would violate the agreement Henryk and I have, but then, the rules don't always apply to Henryk, according to Henryk, so what else is new?

"Would you like to come in?" I ask. "Henryk is away and I'm looking after Karol."

The door closes behind him. He stands in the entrance hall. "Are they true, teacher, your stories?"

"Come through to the kitchen," I say, thinking of an answer. Maybe the answer he wants.

I don't need to ask how Gael knows Henryk.

"Teacher, how do you know Henryk?" Gael asks.

"Oh, you know, we're old mates," I reply. "And you, Gael, how do you know Henryk?"

118

"Oh, you know," he says. "We're new mates."

"Would you like a beer?" I ask as we enter the kitchen.

Karol the old Labrador crooks an eyebrow from his bed in the corner, then lumbers up and crosses to Gael for a pat.

"No, thank you. I would like something else, Paul." He smiles, tickles Karol under the chin, pulls his tank top off over his head, and throws it on the benchtop. "I was very happy to see you on this street yesterday, riding on your cycle."

Gael's blue tattoo starts on his shoulder, a planet, then descends into a meteor spray down his arm, finishing with three stars on his bicep just above his elbow. I am not much into tattoos but wonder what this means.

"My tattoo does not mean anything," Gael says, eyeing me eyeing the tatt. "I just like the design. You can touch it, if you like."

Holding his arm out, I touch the tattoo with my fingertips.

"Grip it," he says. So I grip his arm. He tenses his bicep. "You like Top or bottom?" he asks. "I like both."

"Me too," I say, meeting his gaze. "But if we're gonna fuck, I want you to fuck me." I drop his arm, slip my arm around his waist, feel his naked skin on my forearm, squeeze his arse. "I guess you know the way to the bedroom."


I've shared Henryk's bed with other men before, but only when Henryk was there as well.

So this is new, I think, as I pull my t-shirt over my head and drop it on the floor. Gael is an adult and a sexy one who clearly knows what he wants, but while I've fucked and sucked and rimmed and kissed and pissed as a Top or btm or both with many many many many men, I have never had sex with a (former) student before.

Gael sits back on Henryk's bed and I straddle his lap, kiss his soft lips, kiss his soft lips softly, kiss his soft lips long, savour their taste, slide my arms around him and pull closer, open his mouth with my tongue.

He breathes out, giggles, sighs as my tongue explores his. He pulls away, whispers, "I have never had sex with my teacher before."

"I'm not your teacher anymore," I reply, huffing his scent, pushing him flat onto the bed, pinning his arms above his head while I nuzzle his neck, kiss his collarbone, lick his nipples. He shakes my grip and pulls at my shorts, so I reach down and shuck them off, shuck off my jocks, as he pulls his own off and we pull back the bed covers and soon we're both lying naked together and legs entwined and kissing and touching. He has almost no body hair. I more than make up for it, even with all mine clipped.

Gael caresses my arse as we kiss, delves between my cheeks and searches for my hole.

"I have dreamed of fucking your arse since the first class," he says, licking my ear, nibbling my earlobe. "I want to fuck you now."

So I reach over for the lube, splurge some on his fingers. I lie back, pull my knees onto my chest and he lubes me up, fingers working deftly into my hole. Shuddering with each touch, the lube cool and silky, his fingers smooth and sure. I like that: he was so quiet in class but here he is so confident, taking charge of getting what he wants. And I want to be a generous citizen.

As I clasp my knees, he kneels up, framed between my legs. His hard cock stands proud. It's a little thick, wet with pre-cum, his balls perky underneath.

He smooths just a little lube on the shaft of his cock, then spits on his hand and rubs that in too, so practiced and skilled. He smiles a shy smile that melts my heart and certainly melts any lube swilling in my hole.

He plugs his cock in, head sliding easily inside my welcoming hole, just past my sphincter.

"Easy," he murmurs.

"Very. But now comes the hard part."

He pushes in deeper. Missionary is my favourite, very favourite, most FAVOURITE position to be fucked in.

Love looking up as the Top towers over me.

Love being pinned down by another man's body.

Love the penetration and feeling of tradition, like millions of men before me, on their backs, giving their bodies up to men who want to fuck their souls into oblivion.

And I can't help but fall a little in love each time a hot new Top fucks me in missionary, eyes wide, enjoying the rhythm of his manmeat sliding, gliding, riding me, in and out and in and out and in and out of my fuckhole.

He pinches my nipples, rests his hand on my hairy stomach, claiming my body as he stakes it with his cock. I breathe out, watch his face, so handsome I see now, in and out and in and out and in and out and in and out.

I whisper, "How long have you been planning today?"

"For ... ever," he says. Smiles. Lays a finger over my lips, looks at me, looks into me, looks deep into me.

Breathe in. Breathe out. In and out and in and out and in and out and in and out.

He picks up the pace, quickens each slide in and pull out, works up a rhythm, looks at me, watches me, eyes glazing, sighs. I wonder, when he started, first imagining, his cock, deep inside me (deep and deeper, deep and deeper) so I clamp, my sphincter, tight and tighter, squeeze his cock, he bends forward, and kisses me, kisses kisses, breathes and kisses, tongue and lips, lips and tongue, starts to chant, coos in my face, "Your arse is mine, your arse is mine, your arse is mine, your arse is mine."

My head fills with Gael. I grab his shoulders, pull him close, into me, he owns my hole, his cock so so so so deep deep deep inside me (how can his cock have grown so big?) and I welcome him, a recent arrival to this country, showing him how much we (and me especially) care for him and his future and his heart and his cock with each thrust, each fuck, each push deep into my guts.

"Cum."

His face twists as he gazes, breath quickens, stomach shudders, sphincter tightens, throat groans, cock pushes ... push ... push ... push-errrrsssss into me ... and floods floods my hole with his cum his cum ... cum ... cum ...

Hot sticky cum pumping deep inside me …

He breathes out. Collapses next to me. Spent, chest heaving, eyes closed. Cock wet and cummy.

My hole gapes, spasms, clenches with pleasure and exhaustion and manjuice.

"Ooh," I say, "amazing fuck!"

"Teacher," he whispers, "now can you give me a higher mark for my assignment?"

# HENRYK

# I MAKE A PORNO

Arms slip around my waist. He kisses my neck, licks my ear, manhandles my balls in my shorts.

"Henryk," I sigh. But I like him fondling my package.

We're the same height; same rangy build. Greying cropped beard; body hair pruned and tweezered. And we've had an on-off thing (mostly off) for 30-plus years.

"Y'know you want to, Paulie," he coos. Strokes my hard-on.

"You used the 'F' word, Henryk. You asked for a *favour*." Still hard, balls roiling in their sack, I pull away from his clutch. "And you just called me 'Paulie'."

In our "on" phase 33 years ago we were Commerce students at uni. Now he's a Professor of Statistics, and I run a one-man accountancy business from my home. But we connect at times. We fuck (handy we're both Vers); meet for dinner; go on cycling tours. But if there was ever the-one-who-got-away ...

I'm not talking a white picket fence and a subscription to *Happy Homemaker*, but if we were dead serious, I'd hang up my jockstrap, poppers and online hook-up accounts and shack up. With him.

But it's not gonna happen.

Because Henryk's also always looking out for ways to get rich, not necessarily in a scrupulous, law-abiding, non-exploitative way.

"It's a surefire success." Henryk swigs straight from the bottle of red he brought over to discuss his latest get-rich-quick scheme. "The market research is all there. 'Slav Slaves' has 'winner' written all over it. Winners are grinners."

Henryk may be a brilliant stats boffin but he's a shit business entrepreneur.

"Bingeing on Eastern European porn for 2 months is not market research. Why set up a pornsite when you know nothing about making porn or internet start-ups?"

But the thought of hot fucks with some of Henryk's international students from Slovakia and Hungary and the Czech Republic (and I picture their tall, lean bodies; long, muscular cocks; musky, low-hanging swingers) puts some spring in my pencil.

And Henryk knows my weakness for hung young studs with limited English and a faraway I-need-guidance look in their eyes.

"What are his stats?"

"Andrej's cock is 8 inches. 9 when he's leaning forward."

Later I ask Henryk, as he searches his phone for full body pics of Andrej, "What's this movie's name?"

"*My First Time.*"

Henryk sits. Flick flick flick.

"Original. And the plot?"

"An older guy wants to try man-on-man action. So he gets fucked."

"Can't it be a bit more … literate?" I ask. "More stylish?"

"Porn is cock and balls, cum and holes, Paul," he adds. "You gonna stop halfway to pull out *Jane Eyre* ?"

Henryk hands his phone to me. Andrej has a long cock; flat abs; broad shoulders; a pale dusting of body hair; short, light brown crewcut; smiling at the camera under high cheekbones. Boner-inducing.

"What'll my porn name be?"

Henryk grabs the almost empty bottle of red. "Dick Cavern," he says, then sips, looking at me for a reaction.

"Dick Cavern," I repeat. "It has a ring to it."

*Dick Cavern's First Time*, I wonder? *My First Time in Dick Cavern? In and Out of Dick Cavern?*

*

Two days later. I half-want, half-don't-want the 6.00pm shoot to be called off. I'd planned to complete annual tax returns for a local butcher and his wife (I had a few sessions with the butcher two months ago!) but the dollar signs blur on the computer screen and the decimal points melt off the notes I made.

I'd jerk off but I need to save my cum for the shoot.

I'd have a beer but that'll bloat me and if the camera adds 10 pounds, what's a beer or two gonna add on top of that?!

Hope he's not a bad fuck.

Hope I'm not a bad fuck.

This would be easier if it were a threesome, Andrej and Henryk and me, kissing and fucking and rimming and sucking and cumming. Maybe I should suggest –


6.00pm rolls around, and Henryk is working the camera on a tripod in my bedroom. Lights are placed about the room. It looks professional. But it's Henryk so it's probably cheap.

Andrej sits on the edge of my bed. I sit next to him. Naked. Our legs touch.

"Don't cum until I tell you to," Henryk interrupts for the 27th annoying bossy demanding time. "Save your cum for the money shot."

Henryk is saying 'shot' a lot. Money shot, establishing shot, wide shot, two shot, shot reverse shot, medium shot, long shot, cowboy shot, tracking shot, dolly shot, high angle shot, low angle shot, bird's eye view shot, and others I recognise: medium close-up, close-up and extreme close-up.

It's the close-ups I'm hanging out for.

Andrej's leg presses against mine. I press back. My hands are itching – so is my mouth – to get onto his delicious cock. It's even better in person, long and meaty, uncut but half-hooded. Smooth athletic knackers and a sparse bush.

127

His cock rests on his balls, breathing, easing a little up then easing a little down as he sits – as we both sit – as we both wait – for Henryk to finish whatever Henryk is doing. His cock rocks, shifts, sleeping, maybe even snoring, contemplating.

I can struggle taking really thick cocks but I'm a total fucking champ taking really long cocks. So I'm looking forward to Andrej's cock deep inside me.

"I had an examination today, I am very tired," Andrej says.

"Are you okay?" This seems the right thing to ask. Examinations are intimate but we're about to be incredibly intimate, so I hope my question sounds caring.

"Three hours in a biiiiig buiiilding" – he throws his arms wide in explanation, grazing my nipple – "and I write 20 pages about my knowledge of data collection and exploration, probability, and inference, and using statistical methods to calculate the probability of outcomes."

"Are you ready yet?" I ask Henryk.

"Almost, I just – "

I reach between Andrej's legs and grab his balls. His lips are on mine, tongue probing my mouth, hand gripping my cock.

"Fellas – " Henryk says.

I'm on my back, sliding up the mattress, Andrej and his bouncing meaty fuckstick in hot pursuit of my hungry hole. I spread my legs, throw my ankles in the air. Andrej pushes my knees onto my chest and his tongue darts into my manhole, opening it up, digging like a pneumatic drill.

"Fellas – "

My rock-hard cock bounces against my stomach as Andrej pushes my hips up, tongue driving deeper into my hole. He grabs my balls and squeezes hard – fuck I LOVE that! – grips them, clenches them, squeezes them, squashes them – so I gasp, cry out, moan. I'm supposed to be Dick Cavern, man who's never had man-to-man fun before, but who knows where the fuck Dick's gone 'cause it's me in my bed with Andrej and he's taken my balls prisoner and I'll follow my boys wherever he takes 'em.

"Fellas!"

Andrej snaps in Czech. Henryk spits back in Polish. Andrej's wet wet wet cockhead slides up to my manhole and throbs, poised, so I breathe out, open my gape further. Andrej slides his cock inside me, instant and deep and taking no prisoners. Any worry and concern about this fucking porn shoot explodes out of the top of my head and I brace myself for a momentous cockride.

My legs fold under Andrej's long lean body as he envelopes me, kisses me, presses heavy on top of me. He whispers in Czech, hot in my face as he looks deep into my soul, tool driving into me – into me – into me – into me. He picks up speed. In and in and in and in and in. Up and up and up and up and up. Deep and deep and deeper and deeper and deepest.

Henryk says something but Andrej powers on, cock sawing into my hole, a meat piston, fuck turbine, rutting excavator staking its claim in my guts.

Henryk says something else. "Turn over," Andrej whispers. He pulls out, I flip over, present my hole to him again. He buries his tongue inside, sucking out the arsejuice, then spits on it, shunts his driving tool into me again.

Not a big fan of doggie. But I love bulldog: the Top gets behind and above your hole and glides, slides, rides you so deep it's like his cockhead's going to burst through your throat and coat the roof of your mouth with hot cum.

Andrej slides in behind me, hips pivot so he's also above me, works my hole. It needs meat, craves cock as he drives down down deep into my stomach. Grip my sphincter tight. Andrej moans, low-hangers banging my perineum with each thrust, stab, ram into my thankful, grateful, greedy fuckhole.

Andrej grabs my throat, jerks my head back. My back arches. He grinds for the final stretch.

"FELLAS!"

"Join in or fuck off!" I growl.

Andrej's meat slams into me. SLAM, and SLAM, and SLAM, and SLAM.

"SAVE IT FOR THE MONEY SHOT!"

I want Andrej's cum filling my belly. And SLAM.

My ring tightens, ringbarks Andrej's cock. He moans. I squeeze tighter. Andrej groans. I slacken my grip then wring down, in, on his cock and – and – and – Andrej cries out, guttural, from the base of his balls – and spasms, jolts, shudders, pulses, empties into me. Deep inside my hole. Deep and deep. Deeper and deeper. Deepest. Filling my arse with hot mancream. I feel each flow – ebb – flow – ebb – ebb ...

Andrej pulls out, licks my spent hole.

"Where's Dick Cavern?! You turned into Paul fucking Swallows!" Henryk rages.

"It was Method acting," I say, flopping on my back beside Andrej. I squeeze my sphincter, storing Andrej's deposit safe inside me. "I was in the moment."

Andrej rolls off the bed, cock red and limp. "I have another examination tomorrow. I must go home for study."

Henryk throws his hands up, stomps out, slams the door behind him.

I breathe out, relax into the mattress. And my arse releases a squirty cum burp, splurting over the white sheet.


Later, Henryk says, "There is enough to edit something arty together. That will make you happy: you're the big winner in this fiasco, Paulie."

Sure. Winners are grinners.

So, if you troll the net and see a porno called *Dick Cavern's Quick Fuck*, it's definitely hot. It's definitely real. And it's definitely me.

# GROOMING

"Suck my cock."

A smirk crosses his tanned face. He lies in bed, dressed in a cotton bathrobe, fetchingly open just below the crotch.

It's tempting.

Henryk and I go way, way back, when we were kind of a couple in our 20s. And we sometimes fuck (usually after a few wines). He is, you might recall me saying, the one who got away. If there was ever someone I'd settle down with …

But today, I laugh. He's all handsome smile, short greying beard matching the clipped greying chest hair poking above his robe, arm crooked over his head, fingers waving hello-goodbye.

"I should bring you this close to cumming." I indicate a hair's breadth between my thumb and index finger.

"And you'd leave me hanging too, Paulie," he chuckles. "Fuck, I hate being like this!"

He looks down at both legs fully cast in plaster, up to the groin, in the summer heat. After a car accident that like a lot in Henryk's dodgy life, doesn't add up.

I usually don't ask.

Flashes of metal and colour blur past the window, followed by the sound of a vehicle braking in the driveway.

"You expecting visitors?" I ask.

"The pet groomer. Karol's out the back."

Karol is his Labrador, named after the old pope.

Through the window, I watch a stocky bloke in khaki shorts and shirt, shaved head and longish ginger beard, bound out of a Suzuki

Jimny. He bounces around to the side of his trailer, opens the trailer door.

"She only does cashies. My wallet is – "

"It's a bloke," I cut in.

"Fuck! Now I won't be able to see him."

"He's not your type, too nuggetty," I say.

The pet groomer walks across the front lawn unravelling an electrical cord. He plugs the cord into what must be a socket, under the window, and standing up, sees me watching.

He smiles, waves.

"What's he look like?" Henryk asks.

Hand in my pocket, I feel a familiar stir in my shorts. "He's a ginger, too."

Henryk shrugs, no longer interested.

I head for the door. "I'll get Karol."


"G'day mate," I say, sticking my head through the doorway of the grooming trailer. The trailer's fitted out with a dog bath, grooming table, pipes and hoses, a fan, and an array of pet products in glass-fronted cabinets. "You ready for the dog? I'll just get him for you."

The ginger smiles at me, nods, looks me in the eyes as he uncoils a hose. He's nuggetty, solid, a muscly bantam, on the shorter side but packing a punch in his khaki shorts. Thick ginger chest hair peeks above his shirt. Green eyes. Beard enough to more than tickle any arsehole.

He cocks his head. "We met before, mate?"

He sizes me up and down. Pressures a finger against the end of the hose: a jet of water shoots into the bath.

"You ever drink at the Royal?"

Hands dip into my pockets again. I rock up onto the balls of my feet, press my groin forward, then rock back onto my heels. "Tuesday nights, sometimes," I say.

"That's where I seen you." His fingers grapple with a tap. "In the back car park."

A smile flushes my face at the memory. "Yeah, the one down the lane."

"I don't usually do this run," he says. "The wife does. Mate, you wanna hop in and close the door?"

I'm up that step in no time. Closing the door behind me, I turn to see the unexpected: shirt opened, he's sunk to his knees.

Am I disappointed? Those blokes in the Hotel Royal back car park are so masculine, so butch, reeking of testosterone and Y-chromosomes and machismo. They aim arcs of golden piss into scruffy leather workboots and pound manholes into submission over the hoods of old Ford Fairlanes.

"You wanna flop yer cock out?" he says, green eyes looking up at me. "The wife's gonna have me tea on the table at 6.30."

"Sure," I apologise.

But he wastes no time taking charge, pulling down my shorts then ripping down my jocks and clapping his lips around my cockhead.

I see a wet patch on the white cotton.

As he sucks me down, his right hand cups my balls as his left traces up my thighs, hovers just under my arsehole. I'm not sure what he plans, but his tongue works overtime on my cock, licking the shaft, slicking it with spit, caressing the piss slit, lapping my pre-cum. He releases his mouth-hold on my cock, looks up.

"Grab me fuckin' head."

I grab his head, push his face and his mouth back onto my cock, shove it in deep, spear his fucking tonsils. He chokes, splutters, snots against my short pubes but keeps at it anyway, huffing deep on my meat.

With a throatful of cock, he repositions his hands on my arse, pulls me further into him. I wedge deep inside. He can't get enough fuckstick, throat muscles snapping around my pole, closing and opening, submitting but controlling. He gags again, twice, three times, convulses against my groin, then madly pulls away, saliva streaks roping from his mouth to my cock.

133

"Fuckin' amazing cock," he says, eyes glassy, sniffing, grin broad on his face.

I must have a puzzled expression because he stands up, wipes the ropes of saliva on his sleeve. "What's the problem?"

"Ah, no problem," I say, as he pulls my t-shirt up to my collarbone and tweaks my nipples.

"Mate, I like cock, I like cum, I like holes, I like piss, I like blokes," he adds. "And I get me jollies where I can." He bites my left nipple while pinching my right.

The pleasure is mine as his teeth clamp down, pain shooting up my body.

He sticks his tongue inside my mouth as his fingers work both nips, tongue chugging tongue, heavy-breathing, lips gnashing, throat opening, saliva thick and hot and wet.

He turns around, kicks off his shorts, bends over the bath in his jockstrap, opening up his furry ginger arse.

My fingers part his cheeks, find his hole. He leans back against my hand, squirming as his pucker welcomes my fingertips.

"I cleaned up before 'cos I had a hook-up earlier," he grins. "All you'll find in me arse is Top sprog."

Finger pushes up inside his open, slippery, warm, willing hole.

"Bury your cock in me arse."

I slip a second finger inside –

"Now, son!"

He pulls his shirt off, sinks his head down over the side of the dog bath, sticks his arse out further.

"No lube. I like it natural."

I like a bit of friction, but no lube? Though if there's sprog inside him still …

I spit on my hand, slick my cock up, press my knob against his pucker. He pushes back, relaxes his hole, arse lips swallowing cock … and he rides me, pushing back and opening up and pulling away.

Then pushing back and opening up and pulling away.

Then pushing back and opening up and pulling away.

"Dump your swimmers in me cunt," he says.

He bears down on my cock, tightens his sphincter. I grab his hips, yank him back, bury my tool inside him, up his arse, deep up his fucktube, dropping my pelvis so I get in and under, pulling him back and down. He grips the side of the dog bath, and we're rocking, rutting animals in heat, sweat pouring down my face, his back glistening, my cock pistoning in and out of his hole, him grunting and me groaning and the trailer bouncing, axle squeaking. I dunno how long I can –

"Gimme yer sprog!"

So I do. Grip my glutes and shove deep inside him again, wrap my arms around his bent over body, drive into him with a – a – a – a – grrrrrunt and empty … emp-ty … empppp-tyyyy my cum … into … his guts.

Yeah …

I pull out, cock slick and wet with cum and arsejuice and maybe the earlier hook-up's sprog. He's still bent over the dog bath. I kiss his glistening back, lick up his sweat.

He rights himself, forces me to stand up too. Facing me, "Nips," he says. Pulls down his jock, grabs his cock. I twist his nips as he jerks his meat, press – grind – crush his nips under my thumbs as his eyes bore into me, chin set grim, cock-grip furious.

His whole body tenses, rigid, then a rush, a sharp breath gasp – ah – hah – chest contracts and the release, sperm shoots out his slit, sprays my thighs and pubes and cock, pulsing protein, milky and sticky and – I slide my fingers through it – warm and white and tasty.

Then quick as a flash he's shoved the hose up his hole, wrenched it on, eyes glazing over, back arching, grin on his face as he rocks back and forth and his arse fills with water. Then pulls the hose out, hoicks his arse over the rim of the dog bath, and jets a spray of water out of his hole.

He shoves the hose back in, moans as he fills 'er up again. Mesmerised, I watch as – grimace, sigh, eye roll – he pulls the hose out again and shoots his cummy guts into the bath.

He glares, fierce and wanting so I grab his nipples again and squeeeeeze. He cries out, shoves the hose in, fills up, hose out. I ease the pressure on his nips, and a slower, more artful stream, more sphincter control, more sighing release ... dribble ...

He twists off the tap, throws the hose in the bath. Laughs, wipes his forehead with his arm.

"You got a talented arse, mate," I say.

"Thanks. But don't tell the blokes at the Royal."


"Hey Paul, did you fuck?" Henryk calls out.

I'm leading Karol through the house, ready for his doggie wash.

"I saw you disappear into the trailer. Then it started to rock."

"Nah. Not today," I answer.

But reaching into my pocket, I feel the thickness (and the promise) of his business card.

# BACKSEAT BUKKAKE BLISS

I have long loved beautiful cars. The beauty of a white 1936 Cord 810 Phaeton Convertible (go on, look it up on the web now!) is mesmerising. I know. I saw one in person and stood for ten minutes, gaping at its incomparable beauty.

Or the 1937 Mercedes-Benz 540 K Cabriolet.

Hands-free orgasm.

So, I'm in Stuttgart in July. With Henryk, "the-one-who-got-away", who I had a short relationship with in our 20s, when we were both Commerce students at uni. Whose conservative Catholic upbringing kind of got in the long-term way.

We still fuck, at times. And travel together. Do each other favours.

Henryk spent two weeks in Poland, visiting relatives, then flew to Berlin then trained it to Stuttgart to meet me. (I flew in from Rome.) We have separate rooms at the Park Inn on Hauptstätter Straße but on the same floor and meet when the need arises.

The city centre of Stuttgart had the shit bombed out of it during the war, so it is not the most beautiful of cities: very post-war, build-'em-quick, 50s-60s-70s not-so-gorgeous.

But I'm not here for the architecture and the cosy neighbourhoods. I'm here for the Mercedes-Benz Museum.

Our visit is scheduled for Sunday.

We ride from the museum's granite ground floor to the top of the building, in one of the three Art Deco-Space Agey lifts, then wind our way down a slow spiral over many floors, from the earliest horseless carriages to the latest prototypes. The 1937 540 K Cabriolet is somewhere in the middle.

I could rush through the museum until I find it, but I do not want to spoil the surprise.

But I know I know I know it is here.

I keep looking, on each floor, after each turn and every ramp …

And yes! Finally, there it is! – pillar box red exterior paint and the interior a buttery yellow leather. 4-seater 2-door. Shiny but serious chrome. Circular headlights, Mercedes star atop the grille. Bakelite steering wheel (or ivory), glowing white and chrome dashboard. Slung low, with a sloped boot dipping to the ground.

Incomparable beauty.

I want to run my hands over it, sink into the leather seats, polish the dashboard chrome with my own spit. I'm having an orgasm just gazing at it. But we have to stand back; look, not touch. It's a museum we stand in, not a steamroom.

"Oh oh oh oh oh, it is so heavenly," I whisper to Henryk. "Oh, to be fucked in the backseat."


Henryk has arranged a mystery outing Monday evening. "Wear your white cycle shorts," he tells me. "I'm wearing my pale blue ones."

Not a lot of info and a lot of inconvenience, this outing is typically Henryk.

We catch the S-Bahn to Neckarpark and backpacks slapping against our shoulders in the evening air, walk to the Museum again. (The same trek we took yesterday, in the daytime!)

"It'll be fun, you'll see," Henryk jokes.


The thing is, most museums in Germany are closed on Mondays.

Arriving at the front of the magnificent museum building, with its sensuous buff-grey metal and glass curves, like a sexy alien circus tent awaiting showtime, we walk around the back of the building, cross a courtyard, and wait outside a low-lying bunker beside a door with 'Sicherheit' painted on it in small letters.

I don't ask Henryk why we are doing this. But it's his usual, I assume: dodgy as. The only hint is, when we met in the hotel foyer, he lightly touched the bulge in my white cycle shorts and said, "Nice package, hope I get to snack on it soon."

So, who knows ...

The 'Sicherheit' door opens.

"Tomasz?" asks Henryk.

"Tak," says Tomasz. They shake hands and start speaking rapid-fire Polish. (Of course: Henryk can spot a Pole a mile away!) We're soon following him through the door and down some stairs and along a corridor and under the plaza we just walked across (I think) and into the bowels of the museum proper.

It's only once we're up in the granite ground floor foyer (now looking much larger than when it was filled with people yesterday morning), that I see Tomasz properly. Figure-hugging black cargo pants that sculpt his arse; black boots; wide shoulders under a tight ribbed jumper (it's much colder inside than out), 'Sicherheit' sewn down one arm.

Tomasz takes us upstairs in one of the Art Deco-Space Agey lifts, then leads us through the dim light, around a partition and past display cases and a lot of gorgeous Mercs directly to ... the pillar box red 1937 Mercedes Benz 540 K Cabriolet. Its buttery yellow leather looks so soft and inviting.

Henryk smiles, slips his arm around my waist and says, "Hop in."

Tomasz clicks open the passenger door and pushes the seat forward. I step up and sink into the back seat. The leather is soft and luxurious, velvety and doughy under my fingers. The car sits low, my head groin height. I see Tomasz's cock bulging in his cargo pants. He unzips his fly, pulls down his pants and underwear, cock springing forth, swingers to match, rolling in their sack.

He pushes his half-hooded cock towards my mouth, and as I open my lips he slides inside me, slowly ... clasps the back of my head and pulls me into him, pubes deep. Oh man, I taste pre-cum and smell hot manfunk and touch silky knackers.

Henryk slips in beside me on the backseat, grabs the waistband of my cycle shorts and pulls them down, smooth and practiced. My own cock springs out, and Henryk leans over and claps his mouth around my leaking cockhead, flicking his tongue around the crown, lapping the pre-cum from my piss slit, caressing my balls, sliding a finger under my perineum and searching for my hole.

Tomasz wants more attention, so he grabs my ears and starts pushing his meat deep against my tonsils, his balls now swinging free and banging against my chin.

It's hard to concentrate on just one of the men paying me attention. And soon there's another security guy standing watch, rubbing his bulge through his black cargo pants. I take a two-second breather from sucking Tomasz's delicious uncut meat and look up to catch his handsome face, smooth high wide cheekbones over stubble, and blue eyes, and beside him a young cocoa-coloured stunner, wide shoulder and trim waist, who pulls his own cock out and starts stroking. Big smiles from both fellas, and the second bloke steps forward and offers me his uncut cock. It's an offer I cannot refuse, so I open my mouth and take it inside me, suck it deep and long, tasting the pre-cum, licking the slit, fingering his balls. Then it's back to Tomasz's cock, while holding #2's balls, pulling them down as he strokes.

The two security guards slip arms around each other, both pushing their meat in my face, so I swap from cock to cock, lick for lick, suck for suck, grabbing them and shoving both meaty cockheads in my mouth.

Looking up from my mouthload, I watch them kiss, and then realise my cock is now not warmly encased in the mouth of a rangy mate about my age but is wet and standing free.

A quick look behind me and I see another security guard has fallen in, tall and thin and blond and dressed in regulation black, standing beside the 540 K with his long cock busy in Henryk's welcoming mouth. Henryk is an expert cocksucker and punctuates his work with grunts and slurps, sighs and snorts.

I return to my original mission, and clasping both cocks together, work my lips around both so they fill my mouth. I can't do much else, but the men frot their cocks together, both clasping my head so they reach as deep as they can. I choke and splutter and pull away, and I can see that the stunner is close, pulling on his foreskin, jerking his meat, breathing heavy.

I grab his balls again, and sitting back on the set, lie my head back and pull his swingers towards me. His cock is centimetres from my face, peaking, grinding, tightening, straining, and then as Tomasz slaps him on the arse, he cries out and shoots ropes of cum across my face. My tongue darts out as he pumps more hot jizz on my cheeks and on my lips and my moustache, licking up his protein shake as he shudders, wipes his cummy cock on my nose, draws back. I dart forward and lick drops of cum off the end of his cock. He grins, shows his appreciation by clasping Tomasz's arse and pushing him towards my cummy face. And Tomasz obliges me with an extreme close-up of his cock, as he jerks and strains and pumps his meat, balls churning, face sweaty and hot.

And up it cums, a huge geyser of white-hot man sap, over my forehead then down on my beard as his cock lets loose, spraying a wide arc of sticky creamy lust across my face. I stick my tongue out and collect his cream, swallowing it down my gullet, happy to be servicing two hot men with such a minimum of fuss.

As they pull away – and I belch a cumburp – the tall, thin, blond number who was fucking Henryk's face is now in line at mine. He pushes his cockhead past my lips. All this facial action makes we want to turn around and offer up my arse … but I think of the mess fucking might make on this work of Mercedes-Benz art, and not having missed a sprog drop, I chow down on his tasty cock – long and thin like its owner – and within seconds (fully prepped by Henryk beforehand) he pulls back to shoot wads of sprog across my face, too.

Maybe my face looks a little dry under this dim lighting.

He finishes, holds my head as he wipes the last of his cum on my beard. I look up at his broad smile, just as he steps aside and lets another black-clad bloke in, shorter and nuggetty but built too, bantam bodybuilder-type, a shorter girthier cock. He slaps his cock in my face and I feel its sweaty sting. He grabs my head in a crushing grip, nearly wrenches it off my neck as he shoves his cock in my mouth. I gag, choke, sputter, but he holds my head and won't let go. His cock muscles spasm in my mouth, and he thrusts my head away just as he shoots a magnificent sploodge of cum right between my eyes, splattering across my cheeks, running down the crevasses of my nose. He grips my head like a scold's bridle, won't let go, cock throbbing, balls exploding, breath heaving until every last drip drop seed of man cum has been unloaded on my shiny, grinning, glistening face.

He pulls away, and I am ready for a break when Henryk steps in. I know his cock so well, know his hot cock smell, know the wrinkles on his balls and the salty taste of his cum and how his cock feels inside me when he fucks me.

It's a slow wank, but as much for the four hot security guards watching him stroke as for me (or for him). They stand around him, still half-dressed, flaccid but still impressive fucksticks sticky and maybe (maybe) not too far off being ready for another round.

The bantam bodybuilder reaches under and pulls Henryk's balls. He groans in appreciation, puts more of his arse into it, and the four men crouch down as they watch Henryk the master wanker at work, pulling his meat back and forth, tight then tighter, cock straining against his hand as we all wait.

And then the first cumshot and a rising cheer, and then the second and the third and the fourth cumshots hit my face thick and strong and the men all bellow their appreciation. I wipe Henryk's cum off my cheeks, lick my fingers, smile at the hot show we've put on for these hot security guards. Bending down, Henryk kisses my cummy lips

"Happy anniversary, Paulie," he says.

I smile. But have no idea what he means.


On the last S-Bahn from Neckarpark, my face is tight with the dried cum of five men, and I am looking forward to a proper fuck with

Henryk back at our hotel. The promise of the fuck is, apparently, part of my anniversary gift.

Later, when his cock is buried inside my hole and he's kissing me as only two men who know each other like the back of their hand can do, I ask him, "What's the anniversary?"

And he says, as he pulls out past my pucker and pushes back even deeper, "32 years ago you broke up with me for the final time. And here we are, still fucking."

I smirk. Henryk nods, and pushing deeper inside me, moans as my sphincter clamps around his cock.

# RAMMED AT BOTH ENDS

It's just Henryk and me at this beer-n-pizza trivia night, his way of thanking me for house-and-dogsitting for him for 2 weeks while he was in New Zealand. Henryk paid for the beer and pizza.

Probably the oldest men (mid-50s) ever to set foot inside this microbrewery, neither of us is doing too badly: rangy; short hair, trimmed beard and moustache; tanned (Henryk more than me); and we're both cyclists so every extra meatball is gonna show so we watch what we eat. Only two beers each tonight and a long cycle tomorrow to get rid of any beer-and-pizza bloat.

Though the two Master of Statistics students he had organised to join us (eastern European hotties with lengthy cocks, tall slim builds and not a lot of body hair) have bailed.

But we know fuck-all answers to the questions yelled out over the PA system. Formula 1? Spotify? Tik Tok? Who cares?

The background music IS LOUD. And the compere's voice (a hefty timbre that rises deep, deep, deep from his balls) is deafening, penetrating our eardrums, making reasonable thought impossible. His dude-patter is relentless.

BUT (and it's a very big but) the compere dude is hot as fuck! Tight dark blue t-shirt showing off impressive guns; tight mid-thigh shorts showing off toned, muscly thighs; toothpaste grin; short dark hair, cropped beard and moustache (all flecked with a little grey). He knows knows knows how fucking handsome he is. Every stretch, every nod, every step communicates his awareness of his good looks and drop-dead amazingly fuckingly hot body.

So while there are no questions about the Tour de France, the Giro d'Italia, the Tour Down Under or music before 2010, the view of the Questions Desk is a winner.

The scores are tallied after each round but we look away from the scoreboard. (We are not dumb but feel unknowing anyway.) And when the compere dude yells it is time for a 20-minute break, he wanders over to our table and places both fists knuckles-down on the tabletop, rattling our beers. "Everything okay, boys?" he asks, looking at Henryk, then me.

I note the name badge above his left nipple, look him in the eye: "Sure, Brad."

"The brewery wants its patrons to have a good time. If there's anything you need, boys ... "

"No thanks, mate," says Henryk.

"Oh well, toilet break time," Brad the dude says. He heads towards the 'Toilets this way' sign. And that's when I realise, and Henryk realises, that he is one of those hot muscle guys who is all stoic and beefcake and nodding masculinity and then he says or does one thing with a flourish and a smile and a breath a little too long and you think, 'Ha! You can be had!' And the way he turns and walks away ... his meaty arse is crying out for attention.

I look at Henryk and he looks at me. I smile. He smiles. And we count 30 seconds then head off to the 'Toilets this way' sign, too.

The men's toilets are empty. No one stands at the urinal, all cubicle doors are open. But back in the corridor, we see another door. 'Staff Only' it says, and the door is oh-so-slightly open.

We push it slowly, and step into a darkened office admin area. But there's another open door a few metres further. 'Staff Toilets' a sign beside the door says, with a light shining behind it. Slowly closing the first door, we step through dim light to the second, shoes squeaking on the concrete floor, and ten steps later we're inside the Staff Men's Toilets. Standing at the urinal is Brad, cock out, but no piss splashing into the trough.

"Hey boys," he says, and stepping back, shows us what he's holding: a very impressive uncut cock, at half-mast, a drop of pre-

145

cum or piss glistening on its end. It's a major sight: big shoulders, beefy arms, broad chest, cock growing in his paw. "Lock the door," he says. I step back and lock it, and turn to see him on his knees, pulling his t-shirt off his waxed chest and tossing it in the corner.

He sinks back on his heels, hard-on sticking out and up from his shorts. Henryk has already pulled down his shorts and jocks, and I do the same. Brad opens his mouth as he plays with his nips, and his mouth is instantly filled with Henryk's long Polish cock. Brad moans, pulls away, smacks his lips then dives back onto it. I muscle in, flash my cock so he knows I'm ready and willing and able and present, too.

Brad grabs Henryk's balls with one hand and tweaks his own nipple with the other. He works the cock, feasting on it, sucking it down, licking the shaft, throating it, slobbering it with saliva, pulling Henryk's balls closer so the cock drives deeper inside his mouth, gagging him, choking him. It's good to see him not yabbering out loud across the room. I grab the back of his head and push him closer so Henryk's cock scrapes his tonsils. Then he starts bobbing, quick short thrusts of his mouth around Henryk's cockhead, tonguing his knob, under it, hand now working the shaft, jerking it, rubbing it, pulling it, tongue and hand in perfect unison.

Henryk groans, leans back and thrusts his groin forward. His mouth open, as his head dips to the side, I kiss him, tongue in his mouth while the dude works his cock. "Don't hold off," I whisper, "we only have 15 minutes left." And like I've pressed a button, the dude ups his rotating hand magic and Henryk relaxes his straining arse and sighs and groans and starts to nut, creamy thick mancum, spurt after rope after creamy slug, across the dude's moustache and lips and into his mouth. Brad yums it all down, but "I want some, too," Henryk says, so Brad stops swallowing, opens his mouth and there it is, Henryk's thick cum pooling on his tongue.

Brad stands up and Henryk kisses him, open-mouthed, so I watch the creamy manmilk roll around their tongues and lips ... and then Henryk kisses me, sharing the load. It tastes like Henryk's cum, and he is a heavy cummer, so there is plenty of salty cum to share.

And as his cum rolls off my tongue and down my throat, Brad turns around and places his hands against the wall beside the urinal, meaty arse stuck out from above his shorts.

Henryk reaches over, sticks his finger in the dude's cummy mouth then sticks his finger in his arse.

But Brad looks at me and says, "It's clean as a whistle, mate, guaranteed."

So as Henryk pulls his finger out of his arse, I step up beside the urinal, Brad spreads his feet and bends his knees slightly. Spitting cummy saliva on his fingers, he runs them through his sphincter, then pushes out his hole, presenting it for my cock.

"Mount my cunt," he says.

I slap my cock to pump more blood into it, slide my hard meat inside his plucked hole. Brad closes his eyes, snorts with pleasure. We don't have much time, so I start fucking him rhythmically. He moans with each push, so I look at Henryk with concern ... who reads my mind and sticks his hand, four fingers and a thumb, in the dude's maw.

"Shut the fuck up, pussy boy. We've heard enough of your fuckin' voice tonight," Henryk snarls.

Brad whimpers as my cock drives into him.

"Tighten your fuckin' hole," Henryk orders. His tighter ring immediately has an effect, gripping my cock as I groan, driving in deeper, harder, quicker. Brad squeals around Henryk's fingers, which only makes Henryk push his hand further down his throat.

"You heard the pussy boy. Fuck his cunt harder!" Henryk demands

I can't look at Henryk's face. If I do, I'll laugh, so focus my gaze on my cock driving into his smooth, very pretty hole.

But there is not much time left so I grip my glutes and push in deeper, picture my cock exploding inside him, flooding his arse with cum.

Henryk slaps Brad on the arse with his free hand. "Tighter!"

My cock is almost strangled by Brad's hole!

And that hole is truly stunning: porn star perfection, not a blemish, and as I pull out his arse lips are tight around my hard-on, living, breathing, pulsating … it's fucking fucking fucking hot. I feel the surge from the base of my cock. I don't want to cum but we don't have much time but I don't want to cum and his pucker is so pretty picture perfect and I thrust and push and fuck and his hole stretches in and out and he's whimpering with Henryk's fist still in his mouth and I moan and he groans and Henryk slaps his arse and I cum I cum I cum I cum I cum flooding flooding flooding his arse his arse his arse … his arse …

Henryk extracts his fist from Brad's mouth.

I extract my cock from his manhole. Brad shoves two fingers inside, jimmies them around and scoops out cum and arsejuice. He shoves them in his mouth, feasting on them like he hasn't been fed in days. "Mmmm, fuck bad breath," he says, and snorts.

He leans over and kisses Henryk, clamping his mouth around Henryk's tongue. Henryk chugs down all the juice he can, and as he pulls away, cummy saliva streaks between their mouths. Then Henryk kisses me, sharing my load and the taste of Brad's arse and his own breath and fuck, it's time to go, the break is over. Brad pulls up his shorts and pats us on the shoulders and says "Thanks boys" and unlocks the door and we hear his shoes squeak on the concrete floor.


Back in the beer hall, cock still sticky in my jocks, the raucous noise starts again and I count the seconds until we can make a gracious exit.

"Hope you used the break to bone up on some answers," Brad's voice booms across the hall. And looking just past us, he adds, "'Cause I certainly had some issues solved."

# TONY

## AND

# GARETH

# THANK YOU FOR SITTING ON MY FACE

Back and forth, back and forth, back and forth, back and forth – you know the deal. Lots of chat, no fucking action.

Problem is, we've fucked before.

"He is hung like a donkey," Sanjeev had said. "His cock looks delicious."

Handsome, older, gym-fit and on the tall side, green eyes, erect nipples, with a full head of grey hair and a short, neat grey beard. A mat of grey hair on a barrel chest, big low-hanging bulge in his jeans.

"Good to meet you, mate," he'd said when we shook hands, clasping mine in a firm grip.

Fuckingly, ball-churningly, arse-tighteningly hot.

So we keep messaging and chatting. Because I know what I'm missing out on.

But he's being cagey. Something's afoot. Amiss. Awry.

It's many intense messages ... then nothing. Then intense messaging again ... and nothing. Arrangements made, arrangements postponed, arrangements resumed, arrangements cancelled.

Fucking hormonal merry-go-round.

But wait! Suddenly he's here – on my front doorstep!

"G'day mate," he says, stepping inside just as I open the door. "Thanks for persevering."

The grey god Tony. And the big piece of meat swinging between his legs is already half-erect, I can see, tenting his jeans.

"You mind if we get down to it, mate?" he says. "I'm fuckin' horny as."

Man on a mission, he heads down the hallway to the bedroom. About to make a left – that's the guest bedroom, where Sanjeev stayed (and where Tony fucked me while I fucked Sanjeev) – I call out, "It's on the right, mate, my room's on the right."

"Oh," Tony says, and makes a right instead.

I saunter in, lean against the doorframe, watch him sitting on the edge of the bed, pulling off his shoes and socks.

"In a hurry?"

"Just keen as, mate," he says. He stands up, rips off his polo shirt, unbuckles his belt, steps out of his jeans, drops his jocks and yes – that meaty cock is definitely keen as. I'm sure I can see his balls churning in their sack from where I'm standing in the doorway.

Tony sits back on the bed and spreads his legs so his cock stands up and out in all its fucking glory. It's impressive – cut, thick, veiny, girthy, muscly, throbbing, fleshy head, pre-cum on his piss slit, very suckable, incredibly edible, I want it fucking my arsehole right now
…

Pulling my t-shirt over my head, I drop it on the floor. Then sitting beside him on the bed, I lean in to kiss him.

The deal for me is, I know a few blokes who like blow and go. And blow and go has its place. And if I want blow and go, I can call any of those blokes up and get a blow and go any old fucking time.

But I actually like Tony, or I would if I got to know him better. And I really like connecting with the men I fuck, and jeez – I'm in my own house here, there's no fuckin' meter on my bed, I can take my time! And I want to take my time with this man, spend all the one-on-one time I can. Maybe take it a little further, make it a regular thing
…

He kisses me back, lightly, soft lips on soft lips. I rub my hand on his thigh, fingertips a caress away from his ballbag. His tongue darts into my mouth, so I open mine wider and suck his tongue inside. Releasing the suction, I whisper, "How much time do you have?"

He pulls away. "Half an hour," he says. "Maybe forty minutes. My wife is really sick, and I gotta get back."

Oh …

I hadn't picked him for a married man. I can usually tell. It's an attitude, like their home life and even their work life is cordoned off, a no-go zone, and if they really threw themselves into the fucking and the homosex and the man-on-man intimacy, there'd be no turning back. So instead, it's all matey and friendly and hot (because they don't know when / if they'll be back) but non-committal and superficial and guarded.

But the way he fucked me the last time he was here ... hmmm, this guy slipped through.

"I don't usually talk about my wife," he adds.

I don't usually like the men I fuck talking about their wives either, I want to say.

"But you make me so fucking horny," he says. "Every time we message, I have to go somewhere and jerk off."

Ah well, at least there's that, I think.

Tony scoots back on the sheet and lies face up. "Sit on my face," he says. "I fuckin' love that."

I take my time pulling off my socks. Pulling off my shorts. Pulling off my jocks. I fold them neatly and place them on the chair by the door. Picking up my t-shirt from the floor and folding that too, I place it on top of the shorts and the jocks and the socks.

Tony shifts so he's in the middle of the mattress now, giving me plenty of space to straddle his face and lower my hole over his mouth.

But yeah, I'm just ... taking ... my ... sweet time here.

I stand by the side of the bed, reach across and start stroking his hard cock. It's standing upright, at 90 degrees, a fucking flagpole proud and true and strong. I really want that flagpole in my arse. While I'm stroking it with my hand, my hole is twitching and I can already imagine it sliding inside me, balls deep, to the hilt, pubes mashing against my anus.

He smiles at me. "Sit on my face," he says. "I want to eat you out."

Maybe if he rims me, he'll want to move on and fuck me ... I mean, don't get me wrong, I love being rimmed, but an expert rim job just makes me want a big cock inside my arse even more!

I climb onto the bed, place my knees just behind his head so I'm facing away from his cock, and lower my hole over his face. He reaches up and grabs my hips, pulls my arse down, and darts his tongue into my hole. I gasp. I'm remembering how great he was at eating me out last time, me on my back, furiously jerking my cock while he lapped at my twitching, oozing hole with his silky tongue.

In and out, biting the skin around the hole. My pucker's quivering and blinking and opening up for more and he's barely started.

Fuck he's good. He should give rimming lessons; he'd make a fucking fortune.

Then muffled sounds from his mouth. I raise my hips off his face.

"What'd you say, mate?" I ask.

"You got any loads in you?" he repeats.

"Nah, mate, sorry. It's been a slow week."

He pulls my hips back down over his mouth, then grabbing my cheeks, spreads my hole open with his fingers, and really digs in with his tongue. Like if he really digs in, up and in and searching and sucking, he'll find a spare load I forgot was lodged deep inside me. Like his general nutrition and wellbeing demands it. Like he's an anal explorer and won't rest until he's found and swallowed his treasure. Like he's fucking addicted to cumshots felched from willing, gaping, fucked and used arseholes.

Hey, I'm not complaining …

I move my arse back and forth, opening and closing my ring, hoping to squeeze his tongue deep inside me and keep it there, trapped, always probing.

"Fuck, you got a great arse, mate," he says. "I could eat it all day."

But then he shucks down the bed and rolling over, is up on his knees behind me and pressing his extremely hard member between my legs and under my hole.

"I wanted to rim you 'til you came," he whispers in my ear. "But wouldn't you know it, I changed my mind."

His cockhead presses against my sphincter.

I'm wet from him eating me out and I like it sticky, not sloppy ... but I reach over for the lube I always keep by the bed, anyway. Handing the tube to him, he squirts a little on his fingers and works it into my hole. Just a little. Not a lot. So there'll be some friction. My, he's a man after my own heart.

My cock is hard hard hard with expectation. I don't want to touch it in case I trigger my orgasm. So I bend forward and stick my arse out. Tony fingers my hole deeper while tonguing my arse lips. He probes deep and nips around the hole.

"You wanna load me up?" I ask between gasps.

"Thought I might give it a burl," he says.

He kneels up again and pushes his cockhead past my ring. I relax, loosen my grip, allow his pole deeper access. A second later his pubes are mashing against my anus and his cock has found its rightful home. I reach under, between my legs, and cup his balls with my hand. He groans, so I grip them tighter, pull them down and he gulps. I wanna squeeze all the cum I can from his churning nuts so they flood my arse with his tasty swimmers.

No fantasy too high and no reality too low.

He picks up a grinding rhythm, breathing out with each push into my guts.

"I'm not gonna hold back," he says.

I didn't think he was going to – he has a sick wife to run home to. But I wouldn't mind some quality time together before he bursts inside my arse. More than just a pump and –

He groans. Fuck! He's cumming already!

I release my grip on his balls and loosen my ring, hoping it will stem the loadflow.

Hold it! I want to call out.

Ah ... he stops.

Oh ...

No.

He's not cumming.

"Fuck you gotta great hole, mate," he says, cock poised just inside my hole. Waiting.

Slowly he picks up the rhythm again, pushing his meat down inside me, to the hilt, balls deep again, so I feel every millimetre of his powertool almost hitting my stomach. "I could fuck it all day."

(Yeah, but what'll your wife say?)

I push my arse back against him and look over my shoulder. His eyes are closed and sweat's running down his temples and into his short grey beard. I can't help it – he's fucking hot and I want his manjuice lodged inside me.

So I tighten my ring again.

Instant reaction – a long moaning groan. "Fuuuuck …" he says. "Fuuucuuuuk."

His hard, thick, meaty cock starts slamming into me. SLAM and SLAM and SLAM and SLAM.

I push back, meeting him halfway, aggressive hole wanting aggressive cock.

"Fuck me," I say.

"I'm not gonna hold back," he reminds me.

SLAM … SLAM … SLAM … SLAM …

Fuckhole craving fuckstick.

"Fuck me!"

SLAM … SLAM … SLAM … SLAM …

Manhole needing manpole.

"Fuck me!"

SLAM … SLAM … SLAM … SL – and STOPS, cock DEEP DEEP DEEP inside my fuckhole. Then pulls back, almost out of my hole, almost, just inside it … just inside …

He shudders … and shoots. Shoots. Shoots spurts of cum, short blasts of hot cum into me – into me – into me – into me.

I can feel each pump, each pump on my sphincter, each pump spurting into my hole, his nuts churning out manjuice, spraying my fuckhole with short cumspurts, sating my need for manhole attention and hot throbbing meat and sticky mancum.

I smile. Yeah … my hole has done me proud. Clamping my ring around his meat, I grab my cock and pulling the skin back HARD, one jerk, two jerks, three jerks, four jerks on the shaft, groan, moan, head spinning, hunker down and shoot – shoot ropes and ropes of my own load across the pillows on the bed. One … two … three long arcs … … … and four hot cummy dribbles at the end.

But I'm hardly done sprogging across the linen when I realise Tony isn't done yet. He's flat on his back again, pushing his face between my legs and under my fuckhole, opening my arse lips with his fingers and probing tongue, lapping at his load just inside me, licking it out, chugging down his own seed. "Open up," he says, slapping me on the arse, so I relax my hole some more, concentrate on not shuddering with each touch and he's in there, deeper, lips and teeth and tongue snacking on his own man-protein as I clench my gut and push and his seed dribbles out of my arse. "Mmmm," he's moaning, lips smacking, throat swallowing, body tensing. He tongues my arse lips, licking down every last – last – last – last – skerrick of his cum.

Is this the ultimate in self-worship, eating your own cum?

As long as he's eating it out of my arsehole, who fucking cares?!

Tony rolls off the bed, and as I sit back down on the mattress, moist hole sticky on the sheet, he stands up by the side of the bed. He picks up his discarded jocks from the floor, wipes them on his cock and balls, holds them to his face, and sniffs long and hard.

Then, "Thank you for sitting on my face," he says, and touching his stomach, he pulls his head back, tucks in his chin, opens his mouth, and buuuurps.

# EVERYTHING REALLY IS A PENIS

"Out for dinner, using the pepper grinder on my steak: it's like a cock I'm jerking off! In the shower at the gym, I bend over washing my ankles for 5 minutes while I imagine a hung bloke behind me fucking my arse! I love cherry yoghurt but swapped to natural: it's sour and disgusting but it seems more authentic when I roll it in my mouth like a giant wad of cum!"

Sinking a few Friday beers in my garden, he pulls his balls out of his crotch, sits back in the hammock chair, picks up his stubby. When he called this morning, he sounded desperate and crazy. And I often wondered if he had this other side but … fuck!

"After thirty years with the same woman, I'm ready for cock." He chugs his beer. "Can you swing a hot stud who'd go easy on a first-timer: 30s to 50s, toned, handsome, killer cock?"

He pulls at his balls again: a wet patch grows at the front of his shorts. "Trade you for a lifetime of free consultations."

This is my ex-psychiatrist talking! I was his patient twenty-five years ago, when I needed a psychiatrist. We're mates. We have shared a lot. Though he's not like a normal psychiatrist: he's so jovial and direct and immediate, and even more so now, an open book.

I sit back in my hammock chair, sip my beer, observe him: late 50s, tanned, full head of short grey hair, clean-shaven. Toned, takes care of himself, no slacko in the smarts department either. A real silver fox.

"I've been seeing patients for the last two weeks with a dildo shoved up my arse!"

I often focus on his mouth when we talk, wonder what it would be like to kiss him. His lips look so soft and inviting and kissable: pulling him into me, opening his mouth with my tongue, feeling his body tense then melt.

"Talk about repressed! Fuck, I should have gone to therapy!"

So … is this is a task for me?

I look him directly in his eyes. "Mate, I'll break you in. I'll fuck you."

"We're mates, I don't want a pity fuck," he says.

"We'll still be mates afterwards. Me fucking you won't change a thing." I swig my beer again, stand up, let him see the growing bulge in my shorts. Then launch into a short chat about douching.


Gareth talks, soaps up his body. I sit on the toilet, seat closed, naked, watching through the shower door, not listening. Water sprays over Gareth's shoulders, down his chest, across his stomach and back, down his legs. He has a nice cock, lean and surprisingly long, and great knackers swing underneath: meaty, a little hairy, suckable.

"Gotta great cock and nice meaty balls, Gareth."

He laughs. "I'm a bit fond of them myself."

He flicks his cock out, water splashes off the tip; turns the tap off; opens the door, steps out of the shower. I hand him a towel.

"I really *really* appreciate you doing this, mate, but I don't want
_"

"Shut up about the pity fuck. I've never broken in a mate before. This way, we both win!"

I step into the shower, turn on the tap, close the door.


Gareth lies naked on my bed, hard cock bouncing. Half-wet from the shower, I slide onto the sheet, push my knees under his balls, force his legs to spread.

I've NEVER fucked an anal virgin before.

He looks at me, eyes searching.

Holding his balls with one hand, I pick up his hard cock with the other, slowly slide my mouth over his cockhead, lips down the whole shaft, mouthing it, licking it, tonguing his piss slit, tasting his pre-cum. There's a lot of pre-cum: his cock is wet wet wet. And I fucking love the taste of pre-cum.

I always thought Gareth was hot. This is not the first time I have imagined his cock balls-deep in my throat, my meat balls-deep in his arse.

I squeeze his balls, slightly. I know the pleasure of pressure on your knackers. He breathes out, settles into the mattress. "Ooooh, that's so hot," he mutters, eyes fluttering closed. My mouth works up and down his cock, pubes-deep, full-throating it. "That's so hot, that's so hot, that's so hot," he whispers. "Please … "

I pull back, work my tongue around his knob, circling, swirling, exploring, digging into the piss slit with the tip of my tongue, gently pulling on his balls, sending spasms of pleasure up his crabtrail and down his spine.

I reach up, tweak his right nipple with my left hand. He groans, pushes his head back, gurgles in appreciation. My cock throbs with expectation: I want it buried in his manhole.

"Stick your cock inside me."

But first, I want to take it slow, slowly open his fuckhole, millimetre by millimetre, a finger then my tongue then two fingers then more tongue then three fingers then my slow. Slow. Slow cock. I want him aching and wet before I give it to him.

But there is something else I want, too, to kiss him, smell him, breathe as we kiss. I release his cock from my tongue. It bounces against his skin then I lean up, over him, head for his lips and –

"No kissing," Gareth says.

Instant soft-on.

This is a dealbreaker. If I can't kiss, I can't fuck. If I want connection with a man, then I need to kiss. And I didn't offer to break him in because I'm self-sacrificing. I want a passionate fuck.

I look at his hard, leaking cock. His legs are spread and his balls grind in their sack. His nipples are erect and I haven't had a fuck in a week (it's tax time, the busiest time of the year for accountants) and I really want to get my end away. And he's a fucking silver fox, tan skin, trim, and he fucking wants me! (Or my cock.)

Fuck it! I squeeze 2 dollops of lube on my fingers, work them into his hole. He gasps, shivers, throws his knees onto his chest and opens up his cavern of joy for me.

Top or btm, I don't like a lot of lube. I want skin-on-skin friction. And I am fucked off with his prissy no kissing bullshit, too. Two drops are gonna do, for the both of us.

Cockhead poised outside his ring, "Ready?" I say.

"Yeah, mate," he whispers, longing and desperation in his eyes. "Fuck me fuck me fuck me fuck me."

I slide my big fella inside his fucktube. I take his claim of lots of dildo play for gospel, and it seems true: he barely flinches as I push in. He breathes in, hard, but more from nerves and excitement than pain.

"Fuck me fuck me fuck me."

I press my hands behind his knees, holding his legs down and spread so I have the access to his hole I want.

"Fuck me fuck me," he says again.

My pole glides in and out. "I am fucking you, mate, I am fucking you."

"Your cock feels sooooo gooood."

I know it does. I watch the faces of most of the guys I fuck while I fuck them and they are an impressive array of satisfied fuckers.

Working up a rhythm, in out in out in out in out, it feels so good but damn it! I soooo want to kiss him, lean forward to get that larger angle as his body folds on itself and takes me deeper deeper deeper, bury my tongue in his mouth so I'm sampling him at both ends.

And his face is so handsome, needy and wanting and appreciative as he rocks his pelvis and his hole and his heart back and forth, into me with each thrust and away from me with each pull back. How has he not done this before? He's a natural!

He breathes out and in with me too, the backward and forward motion of my cock and his arse counterbalancing the other, like a limitless revolution, a rhythmic shuttle, an endless union. A forever fuck.

He is so crushingly handsome when he smiles. "Thank you, Paul." He grins, he glows. As I lean into him he grabs my shoulders. "I will never forget this."

"Hang on for the money shot," I say, driving my meat home.

I focus on his cock, jerk it as he holds his legs in the air. He takes my cue, starts jerking it, grunting as I pull out of his hole and slam back in past his ring. Jerk SLAM jerk SLAM jerk SLAM jerk SLAM. Our bodies aim for the same goal. Gazing at his face as he jerks, I so want to kiss him as my cock rides his hole, piledrives into him. And he looks so HOT, eyes imploring for deeper, harder, heavier fucking. I can't believe I've kept it up, but this no kissing just makes me want him and his mouth and his arse more.

Gareth jerks and whimpers, eyes wide, mouth open in expectation and surprise, agony and ecstasy. Jaw tightens, nostrils flare, aaa-aah!

A hot sprogshot streaks across his stomach and chest and splashes his chin, a jizzspray like a fucking geyser, a rival to Old Faithful, a gusher flooding the room and his body and my bed, rich and sticky and creamy, scads and scads of thick white cum.

His chest heaves, his stomach caves and I just I just I just want to kiss him, celebrate his orgasm, lips on lips, my tongue down his throat.

So I do the next best thing: cock slipping out of his hole, I lick, lap, suck, eat all his rich thick creamy cum off his chest and stomach, vacuum it up, slide it over my tongue to savour for later.

But hands clasp my shoulders. Gareth pulls me down, kisses me with desperate force, lips opening, tongue darting across mine, snorting claiming sucking down his cum for himself. I collapse beside him, kissing him, pull him close, lost in his mouth and his cum and his smell and his hands and his skin.

"Thanks for being my first," he whispers.

"We need a rematch," I say, tweaking his nipple.

It's a deal. Fuck-training begins next Friday. I will flood his arse with my cum.

Inside the front door, Gareth kisses me, long and deep, lips and tongue, held breath and arms around my waist, boner in his shorts. Then heads out to his car, back to the office for a late afternoon patient.

Standing beside his Jensen Interceptor, he turns and says in psychiatrist mode, "Freud was fuckin' right, you know. Everything really is a penis!"

# CHAIN FUCK

My psychiatrist mate Gareth took his first cock (mine!) like a champ. Now for his second fuck, he wants a threesome, and for me to organise it.

But … if I organise a threesome and the other two really hit it off, will I be left in the cold? 'Caring is sharing' is a great motto when you control the sharing.

But then ball-churningly, arse-tighteningly hot Tony, the handsome, older, gym-fit, tallish fuck god, with green eyes, erect nipples, a full head of grey hair, short, neat grey beard and a mat of grey hair on his barrel chest, messages me.

'You got the best arse to rim, mate. I need to eat it again.'

Fair enough. He has free time between visits to his wife in hospital (I don't ask), so a lot of back and forth starts between me and Tony and me and Gareth. (Plus, I met Tony in a threesome, so know he will be up for it.)

Pics, times, dates and venue ideas fly between us. For two weeks.

Tony has slabs of free time between hospital visits. But Gareth only has slivers of free time between seeing patients. I almost give up. Then a date and time are finally nailed: Wednesday evening, when Gareth has a cancelled consultation and Tony can swing by for an hour.

But the clincher is, not wanting to lose fucktime travelling, the best place to meet is Gareth's psych practice, located on the second floor of a four-storey office block in a leafy inner-city suburb. So Gareth gives his admin staff time off, reminds Security he will be working a little late, and prepares his consulting room (like all clichéd psychiatrist offices, his features a chaise longue) for the fuckdate.

Fuckday: Gareth can hardly breathe. Standing in the middle of the reception area, wringing his hands, unsure what to do, "You think he'll like me?" he asks.

Gareth is the more dominant personality when we're having drinks or chatting, so these nerves are almost charming.

I chuckle, slip my arm around his waist, pull him towards me, kiss him on the lips. He's hungry so he slips his tongue inside my mouth, reaches up and pinches my nips.

"You still got a buttplug in?" I ask.

"Yeah, been there all day. Makes me so fucking horny!"

We've had the 'douched' convo (we both have) and seriously start to kiss, mouths open, sucking down tongues, chewing lips, pulling nips, rubbing crotches … all in the reception area, where Gareth's wealthy clientele usually wait to absolve their neuroses.

There is a knock on the door. Tony is bang on time.

Closing the door behind him, Tony clasps my hand in a firm grip, then says "G'day" to Gareth and shakes his hand, too. Both men have solid handshakes, and this impresses them both, sizing each other up, like they're each measuring the full weight of their cock and balls in their powerful maws.

"Lead on," Tony says, grabbing Gareth's arse and giving it a squeeze.


Naked, we get down to business. Gareth slides onto the leather chaise longue, sits back against the wall. Tony pulls out his meaty cock and standing astride Gareth's legs, grabs Gareth's chin and immediately slides his cock inside his mouth, starts throat fucking him, gripping his head like a vice as he thrusts forward. Gareth chokes on Tony's meat but very soon (so soon he's such a natural!) he takes it all the way. Tony's balls slap against Gareth's chin, meaty and low and thwacking hard.

"You're doin' good, son," Tony says. (He's probably Gareth's senior by 5 years!) "Takin' it like a true cocksucker." (It's undeniably hot, built silver fox face fucking the tanned silver fox.)

Gareth squirms, gags 'thank you'. I reach up between Tony's thighs, grab his balls, and yank. What man doesn't love having his boys played with, pulled down and even whacked around?

He groans, says "More, son," so I pull them tighter, grip them, ringbark them as he fucks Gareth's face. Gareth starts to choke, pushes Tony's groin away, so I drop my grip as thick streams of saliva string from Gareth's mouth to Tony's cock.

"What a fuckin' opener!" Gareth laughs, wiping his mouth. He coughs, eyes glassy, splutters. Tony turns around to face into the room, plants his feet either side of Gareth's thighs again, and bends over, hands on his knees, so his open arse rubs up against Gareth's face. Gareth wastes no time, grabs Tony's butt, pulls his cheeks apart, sinks his nose and tongue in his crack, starts eating it.

I feel like the third wheel here already, as Tony grins with each huff of man scent and arsemeat and buttjuice Gareth soaks up. And he's making a meal of it too, gripping Tony's hips, face buried in Tony's hole, tonguing deep, arse-appetite wild and insatiable.

"Some men are born to it," Tony grins, who sees my half-mast cock (it's turned on by all this arse-eating and throat fucking) and beckons me over. I stand in front of him as he reaches over and grabs my nuts, hard, really hard, really REALLY hard, staring me in the face, daring me to take it.

"More," I say, pulling my groin away from him, stretching the sack. So he grips them, crushes them in his powerful fist. This is fucking painful and fucking hot.

"We need a session with weights on our balls," he promises.

"Yeah," I say, as he loosens his grip and stands up.

"Turn over, son," he tells Gareth. "Kneel over the couch, facing the wall."

Gareth kneels on the floor, over the couch, his arse filled with a black buttplug. Tony pulls it out, revealing Gareth's gaping hole. He hands the plug to me. But Gareth turns his head and looks at it

166

longingly, so I give the buttplug to him. Gareth holds it, looks at it, licks it, sniffs it, stuffs as much of it in his mouth as he can, pulls it out, licks it again. "Fuck that tastes good," he says.

I can't believe how far he's come on only his second fuck!

Tony whacks Gareth on the arse, a stinging smack. Gareth shudders, his gape blinking, opening looser. He looks over his shoulder at Tony, eyes wide and imploring, the buttplug tossed aside, and Tony bends behind him, hands pressing down on Gareth's back as he slowly pushes his cock past Gareth's pucker and doesn't stop, keeps sliding, grunts and breathes out, drives it down his fucktube until his cock is buried deep inside Gareth's arse.

Gareth exhales, a big lung expulsion. "Fuuuck!"

Gareth is in his own world, and Tony's having fun gripping Gareth's hips and exploring the limits of Gareth's arse. And I'm watching.

Being a voyeur is fun, when you want to be a voyeur. So I nip in behind Tony, hands searching for his hole. Tony's always been a total Top with me but stranger things have happened (and I'm a bit pissed off with the way things are turning out) so as he's pushing in and out and in and out and in and out and in and out of Gareth's fuckhole, as Gareth moans with pleasure and cries "Fuck me! Fuck me! Fuck me!" ... Tony suddenly stops, and my prying fingers gain some purchase and his hole opens up.

He says over his shoulder, "I haven't been fucked in a looong time, mate," and as Gareth pleads "Fuck me!" again, shrill and desperate, Tony pushes his arse out and my cock, like sonar, finds its nestling place between Tony's cheeks.

Tony pushes his meat into Gareth, who gulps, then pulls out and pushes onto my cock, my cockhead just inside his hole. It's like I'm fucking them both. As Tony pushes into Gareth then pulls out, with each pull back my cock buries deeper inside Tony's arse, like a chain fuck, a link of men fucking and taking and giving mutual pleasure, thrusting in and pulling out and thrusting in and pulling out and tightening sphincters and driving on and in and up to total mind-spinning oblivion.

"Fuck me fuck me fuck me," Gareth pleads.

"We are buddy, we are fucking you," Tony answers, and we are, we truly are.

Then I change tack, alter the rhythm, push in when Tony pushes in, pull back when he pulls back. So the thrusting increases, the pistoning deepens, the driving hardens. And from behind, I pinch Tony's nipples and pull.

Tony moans with each simultaneous push into Gareth's arse and into his own, and the heat and the sweat and the smell of man sex and Gareth's cries with each thrust and the whole fucking feeling and stink of men and cocks and balls and arseholes and armpits and bodies is so potent and pungent and perfect that we don't hear the click of the door or see, until he's framed in the doorway, a security guard, shaven head, standing tall and muscly in tight dark blue polo shirt and cargo pants.

He coughs.

Three heads snap in his direction.

"I came to investigate a noise," he says.

Fuck! The show we're giving is not illegal but Tony and Gareth have wives. Plus, we all have hard-ons ... and who wants to waste a good hard-on?

The security guard has a very obvious bulge in his cargo pants. Which he rubs.

"G'day," says Tony, offering his hand. The two men shake. And pulling his cock out of Gareth's arse and pointing at his welcoming hole, "Over to you, son," Tony adds.

"Nah thanks, mate," says the security guard. "If you don't mind, I wanna watch first."

And with that, he pulls down his pants, pulls out his hard cock and a rolling set of knackers. Sitting next to Gareth still bent over on the chaise longue, he slaps him hard on the arse and says, "When you're both done, fellas, I'll have a crack at it then."

# THE FUCKLIST

My (ex-psychiatrist) mate Gareth has been doing a lot of research and compiling a list of what he wants to do sexually. He keeps surprising me with what he's found out about and wants to try.

"I want to be fucked at a beat," he says Wednesday lunchtime, on his back, his knees pulled onto his chest. He is between patient appointments and I'm taking a break from completing income tax returns for the local gourmet butcher and his family. (I've been fucked by the butcher, too. Nice meaty cock!) After a lot of kissing and touching and licking (since I broke him in, Gareth wants mansex 24 / 7), I'm now about to sink my cock into his arse.

I lean over to kiss him again. He's a great kisser: lots of soft tongue and saliva and heat. Our semi-regular fucktime is great, the way he has blossomed now he's getting man attention is great and this fucklist he has is great, too.

"I found a good one," he says.

Gareth's research has revealed a beat that works busiest at night, a toilet block in a park that's just off a main road twenty minutes away. I have never heard of the beat before, but when I was a major beat queen the park wasn't there and nor were the toilets.

There's an honesty I love about gay beats. Men are there for only one thing.

It's Friday night and as I swing my VW Golf into the dark car park, I see his Jensen Interceptor parked further up the road. The Jensen is a speccy car, instantly noticeable. If he wants to remain anon, he'll have to use a different car. (He has a four-car garage and five cars, the spoils of his psychiatry practice.)

The Golf's door closes with a quiet click. I step lightly across the gravel but my shoes still crunch as I head toward the toilet block. A delivery van is parked close to the toilets, with a ute (a utility vehicle, or pickup truck to the uninitiated) and a sporty Merc parked further away. No one sits in the cars, so the beat could be busy. Or the drivers may be walking their dogs in the park in the dark.

My shoes scratch on gritty cement as I step inside the toilet block. It smells of stale piss and fetid water and men. In the semi-dark there's my boy, facing the urinal, polo shirt slung over a shoulder, a leather harness buckled across his pecs and back. His shorts are halfway to his ankles and a jockstrap reveals his bare arse. He turns, face tense, then smiles, half-hard cock in his hands. And that's when I see a young bloke, slim and toned and dressed in a tight tank top and shorts and runners, blond and a short beard, squatting in the urinal, leaning back against the splashback. Gareth's been getting in early, feeding the twink his cock. Fuck, he learns fast!

Gareth nods and the twink smiles. I nip in sharpish and fondle Gareth's arse, run my hand up and down his crack, fingers searching for his hole. As he throws his head back and sighs, I reach around and cup his balls with my other hand, stick my tongue in his ear, lick his earlobe and breathe softly on his neck. "Give it to him. He wants it."

"Yeah, I want it," the twink says, opening his mouth. Though what does he want? Gareth's cock, his cum, his piss? Money?

Gareth rocks back on his heels, his head still thrown back, and releases a thin stream of piss. I uncup his balls, in case he somehow needs them swinging and free, and the flow increases, into the piss-twink's mouth. The twink swallows the golden stream, dribbles it down his chin and onto his tank, sucks it down and slurps it out and makes a pissy piggy mess of himself.

This is another on Gareth's list: piss play with a fit twink drinking straight from his tap.

My cock is hard watching the warm piss flow, so I pull down my shorts and jock and start stroking my cock.

Gareth smiles as the piss dribbles to a finish and the twink swallows hard, belching a piss burp that makes me snigger and Gareth chuckle.

I spread Gareth's cheeks and find his hole with my fingertip. His arse is lubed and ready. He bends over slightly, pressing his hands against the splashback above the twink's head, and just as his polo shirt slips off his shoulder into the piss trough, he spreads his feet further apart. I slide one finger, two fingers inside. Gareth does not flinch. He wants it. Expects it. Keeping a buttplug shoved up his arse all day, he has trained his hole hard for this task and he's earned all the attention it gets. He lowers his head, his hard cock and balls swinging free as I grab his hips, poise my cock outside his pucker and slowly enter him.

The twink scrambles up out of the urinal. "Lemme see," he says, and watches as my cock slowly slides past Gareth's sphincter and deep into his arse.

Gareth moans and the twink nods and pulls out his meat, strokes. My hips rock back and forth into Gareth, who sighs like he's been holding it inside forever, like he is finally living his true life.

Gareth's head nods with each slide into him. I look at the harness, ordered from a special leather craftsman, new but buffed and battered to look old and used (no tat for Gareth!) and just as I change tack, release his hips and grab the harness, like I'm riding a fucking horse, we hear a car pulling in near the toilets.

I stop, breathe in, look at the twink (who cranes his head listening) and then pull out of Gareth's hole. The twink pulls up his shorts and darts over to the doorway, tank top wet with Gareth's piss. He walks out.

And returns seconds later, pulling his shorts down again. "I know him," he says. "Seen him here before."

A beefy bloke in his 40s, in t-shirt and jeans and big leather boots saunters in, leans against the wall, grabs his crotch through the denim. He glances towards the doorway, keeping watch, then back at us. He nods, grabs his crotch again.

Picking up where I left off, I step in behind Gareth and hand gripping his harness, push my cock deep inside his fuckhole again, pumping. He squirms, lowers his head, hands steadying against the urinal splashback, seriously into the fuck. The twink drops his shorts to his ankles and standing at the urinal, presses his hands against the splashback and sticks his arse out, too.

The beefy bloke steps up to the task, spits twice on the twink's hole, pulls out his meaty cock and splits the twink's arse with one slick thrust. OOPH! The twink braces himself against the splashback, as the beefy bloke sets to work, fucking the twink's arse with heavy thrusts. And I'm working up a rhythm in Gareth's arse too, my balls slapping against his perineum, keeping pace with the prime fucker. He looks at me as I match him thrust for thrust, grind for grind, grunt for grunt, and the twink grits his teeth and Gareth lets out a sigh so great it almost mists the metal splashback. And the beefster starts wrecking the twink's hole like a fuck machine, like a jackhammer, like a fucking supersonic harpoon.

I start hammering Gareth's hole too, but he lifts his head, signals for me to stop, so I stop, pull out.

But the beefy bloke grabs the twink's hair and pulls him back. He growls, wraps the twink's body up in his arms, pulling him in, pushing into his arse, impaling the twink on his jackhammering cock, each thrust, each grind, each piston a fucking powertool claiming its rightful place inside the young guy's arse. And his hot mouth a gaping silent, grimacing, howling bellow.

The twink collapses against the urinal as the beefster releases his grip and staggers back, his cock dripping with glistening cum. He shakes his head, not quite believing the speed of what just happened, wipes his cummy cock with his paw, licks it hungrily with his tongue, pushes his meat back inside his jeans. Grabbing the twink by the back of the head, he kisses him full on, tongue inside his mouth, enveloping him in his arms again, eating him, sucking him, swilling him down … then breaks away and scuffing boots on gritty floor, is gone.

Gareth coughs. I touch his hole with my finger, slide my cock back inside him. And give the twink time to gather himself together again.

"Tighten it," I tell Gareth, and tensing his glutes, he tightens his pucker and seconds later it sends me over the edge, pumping hot jizz inside him. Filling up with cum again, Gareth breathes out with relief. And I breathe out, a quick breath for each lasting pump, and chuckle, as I so often do when I cum. And pump the very last spurt into him, tensing inside him, squeezing my last cumdrop inside him, my sprog a lasting man deposit in his fucktube. Then I pull out, cock shiny in the half-light.

The twink is on his knees and has my cock in his mouth, cleaning it up, chugging down every last micro-drop of my sprog. I shiver as he tongues my piss slit, clamps the shaft, squeezing the existence out of it as he devours the very essence of life.

"Thanks, buddy," I tell the twink, pulling my cock out of his mouth. He licks his lips, stands up.

Gareth looks puzzled. This is the first time we've fucked where he hasn't cum first.

The twink's cock is hard, a beacon of hope in the middle of the toilet block. I grab it and pulling him with it, lead him to Gareth's arse. I push Gareth's back down and good man that he is, he spreads his feet apart, bends over, relaxes his hole.

The twink takes the cue and as I grab Gareth's harness and pull him back, the twink slides his cock inside Gareth's hole. Even in the semi-dark I see it's a nice muscly cock, and Gareth's moan of appreciation rises deep from the base of his balls. The twink slides in and out, in and out. I help the rhythm for a few pulls on the harness, but then let go, and sink against the wall tired but smiling. The twink's cock grinds into Gareth's happy hole. Gareth jerks his cock, mouth open, groaning, happy to be doing what he now knows he does best.

I grin at the twink. You gotta admire the energy of the young.

Then picking up the pissy polo shirt from the trough, I shove it in Gareth's open mouth. Gareth sucks on it, chugging the cooling piss down.

Now that's another on his fucklist he can cross off.

# DOM

## AND

# MATE

# TOILET TAG TEAM

"Swallow this, son," he says, and beefy arm around me as he leans over from his barstool, hawks a giant gob in my beer – *Ptui!*

The chunky gob floats on the foam.

"Drink up," he orders. "Show a bloke you respect his fuckin' generosity."

I stick my finger in the gob and stir it around the glass. Then I slide my finger inside my open mouth, gob wet and thick and slimy. Curling my tongue, I lick my finger clean.

"Now that's more like it, son," he says, and picking up my beer, knocks it back – throws it down his throat – in one long beery beary glug.

He plants the empty glass down on the bar.

"Thanks for the beer," he says, and grabs me on the back of the neck with his big meaty paw. "I think you're needed somewhere else."


We've been chatting online for a week.

Now, I like connecting with the men I fuck, and conversation over the 'phone can do that … if you give your 'phone number out. (Always eager to do that; nothing to hide.)

But this bloke respects his privacy …

So, I closed my computer today at 1.30, and cycled over to meet him in the front bar of the Royal Hotel at 2.00.

The front bar isn't full – a couple of blokes are talking low, standing at the other end of the bar, and a young guy is playing pool by himself in the next room, watched over by a couple of other blokes – so I found him easily enough, sitting on a barstool, his eyes tracing the tank top muscles of the 20-something beefcake barman. The same barman who's now wiping the bar down having pulled me my beer just two minutes ago. The beer that wasn't ordered by me, or drunk by me, but that I paid for.

Luckily, he looks like his photos, though he's more handsome and rugged in person.

The truth is, he's calling me "son" when I'm probably about eight years older than he is. With a grey short-cropped beard and very short greying hair due to a slowly widening baldspot, I certainly don't look like a "son".

His hair is darker and just as short, and his beard is darker and just as short-cropped.

I'm lean — "rangy" if you're feeling less kind — but I cycle a lot.

He's a muscle bear, though more muscle than bear. Which is really how I like bears. More muscle than bear. But then, you know me, I fuck all types.

Dark hair on his prime beef arms probably stretches across his entire body. (That's what I'm hoping for!)

His dark blue t-shirt, tight across his pecs and biceps, has DOM written above his left nipple, so I take it it's short for 'Dominic'.

Or 'Domenico'.

Yeah, maybe ...

And he has a slight paunch — a sexy, hot, man-in-his-mid-40s paunch — that only adds to his confident masculinity, and his jeans are sculpted more than tight, with a relaxed but heavy bulge in front, resting on the barstool. Hobnail boots on his feet scrape the floor as he stands up.

'Wear shorts and a t-shirt' he messaged, so I did, though not cycle shorts. Short shorts. Easy-to-pull-off shorts. And an easy-to-rip-off t-shirt.

So ...

Game on.

Hand still gripping the back of my neck, he pulls me off the barstool and steers me towards the toilets.

*

The toilets are filthy. They stink. I take a big huff, breathe in deep, the smell of piss and beer and sweat and stale air and toilet blocks floating in the urinal trough and more piss. Fuck! I huff again, a BIG snorting huff. My head is spinning.

Dom steers me in the semi-dark towards the middle cubicle and slams the door open with his fist. Sitting on the toilet is his mate. Naked except for big hobnail boots. Big shoulders. Pierced nipples that glimmer in the dim light. Mate is ginger – I'm hot for ginger, definitely, I'm hot for most things – gripping his big meaty uncut cock in his paws. Another muscle bear. Though more bear than muscle.

Dom releases his hold on my neck and pushes me into the cubicle. "Strip," he says.

As my fingers fumble with the button on my shorts, he grabs them by the waist and pulls them down. I'm wearing a jock – Dom told me to – and despite the stale air in the toilets, my arse feels a rush of cool. He grabs my t-shirt and pulls it over my head, dropping it on the floor.

The floor ... grit scrapes on the soles of my shoes. Puddles of piss spread into the cubicles on either side.

Mate stands up as Dom grinds his boot on my crumpled t-shirt. Good thing I left my designer tees at home.

Dom grabs my arse, pulls it apart, and slides two fingers up and down my crack. He pushes his fingers under my nose. I breathe in deep and smell funky arse crack and man sweat on his fingers, and maybe not just my own.

Dom grabs the back of my neck. "Suck his cock," he says, and pushes me to my knees. And yep, the floor is wet and gritty.

So, I'm kneeling in a puddle of piss, as Mate mounts my mouth with his meaty cock. The knob rasps past my lips and hits the back of my throat. I gag. Clasping my head with his big hands, Mate's cock thrusts hard, in and out of my mouth. He face-fucks me so brutally I give in – resistance is useless – and go with the flow, my head rutting back and forth, back and forth, back and forth as he shoves his cock deep down my throat and down my gullet and probably, if he continues to pound my mouth like a fucking jackhammer, down into my guts. All in a matter of a minute.

Fuck, it's hot in here, I think, wondering what I would be doing if I hadn't answered the call of nature and stepped through the front door of the Royal Hotel at two o'clock.

Mate grinds to a halt, then slowly extracts his cock from my skull. He wipes it against my face – it's covered in sweat, so the pre-cum smears easily – then cupping my chin in his hand, forces me to look up at him.

He grins – Ptui! – and spits in my face.

His gob runs down my cheek. He pushes his throbbing hard-on against my beard, rubbing his spit in with his pre-cum. I smell phlegmy spit and manly pre-cum sweetness as he waves his cock under my nose.

"On your feet," Dom orders.

Placing my hands on the floor to steady me – so they're now covered in piss and grit, too – I stand up.

But before I can look Mate in the eye – sorry, in his face, not his eye! – Dom pushes me forward and grabs me by the hips. Looking between my feet, I see Dom's jeans pushed down to his ankles, and feel his hard cock pressing against my pucker. I give in – resistance is useless – and relax my sphincter as he pushes his throbbing manmeat into my hole.

I love piss.

I love kissing.

I love the humiliating feel of gob on my face, and cum on my face, and arse juice on my face, especially after a dom Top's grabbed my head and pushed and rubbed my face into some hot guy's hot crack.

But cock deep in arse ... arse gripping cock ... you can't beat that for pure animal fucking rutting pleasure.

Mate grabs his cock and stepping aside, leans towards the cubicle wall. Dom pushes me forward some more so I grip the toilet bowl to stop from falling. Peering over the rim, I take another big huff and breathe in the rank smell of what must be stale three-day-old piss. On top of the rank three-day-old piss float two soggy cigarette butts.

When did they allow smoking in the toilets?

Dom is ramming his cock into me, pushing it to the limits of my pelvis. I steel my stance – lock my knees and push the soles of my shoes down onto the floor. He's RAMMING – his COCK – so DEEP – into ME – each THRUST – and SLAM – and THRUST – and SLAM – and THRUST – and THRUST – and THRUST – and THRUST – and THRUST – and THRUST – and THRUST – and THRUST –

I look up as his cock THRUSTS – on REPEAT – on REPEAT – on REPEAT – on REPEAT – on REPEAT – on REPEAT – on REPEAT – on REPEAT ... there are four guys looking down on me, sleazy cheer squad fuckers grinning their fucking faces off, hanging over both walls of the cubicle, two on each side, driving Dom on.

"FUCK him! FUCK him! FUCK him!" they chant. "FUCK him! FUCK him! FUCK him! FUCK him! FUCK him! FUCK him! FUCK him! FUCK him!"

I'd wave and thank them for their encouragement but I'm too busy getting rammed.

Maybe if they'd shut up, I'd ask them to gob on me, too.

I breathe in to focus on the ramming cock inside my arsehole and look into the toilet bowl. With each THRUST of Dom's powercock, the soggy cigarette butts ripple on the surface of the three-day-old piss.

Mate pushes his cock towards my face. I expect to see cum ... or pre-cum ... or dried jizz ... but what I see in the dim light is beads of piss. Little yellow drops. I open my mouth – it seems the right thing to do – but just as I'm about to close my eyes and savour the warm salty flow of ginger muscle bear piss, he shoots his stream off to the right and aims at the toilet paper holder instead.

He soaks the toilet paper with his golden piss.

"FUCK him! FUCK him! FUCK him!" they cheer. "FUCK him! FUCK him! FUCK him!"

But I'm mesmerised by the huge, long, sulphury, beautiful arcing stream of piss.

THRUST – and THRUST – and THRUST – and THRUST.

What a fucking waste! I shake my head as Dom's cock continues ramming my arse. All that gorgeous hot piss wasted on a fucking roll of toilet paper!

Soon the roll is so drenched, Mate's piss drips onto the floor. I stick my tongue out in the hope that somehow, even with Dom's THRUST – and THRUST – and THRUST – and THRUST, I can lean over and catch piss drips on my tongue. I angle my shoulders towards the sodden, soggy toilet roll.

Dom grabs my shoulders, setting them straight. Then giving an almighty GRUUUNT, he shoots his load into my arse. My hole is so sensitive I feel each pulsating pump of hot sticky muscle bear cum.

It's pulse – pulse – pulsing into me.

I lock my knees again and grip my hole around his meat. I've lost out on all that piss, so I don't want to lose a drop of Dom's cum.

Pulse – pulse – pulsing.

Hot cummy goodness.

Pulsing.

My manhole is flooded …

Puls-ing … pul …

… with hot cummy dom goodness.

My hole feels the raspy slide of Dom pulling his cock out.

I peer over the edge of the toilet bowl and smile at the cigarette butts floating on the old piss. My arse feels incredible. Gaping and sore and exhausted and used and red and raw.

Dom's breathing is heavy. I look over my shoulder and see him leaning against the open cubicle door, chest heaving, sweat running down his face, cock glistening with my arse juice and his cum.

Normally I'd suck the Top's cock clean but I've got most of his cum still deep inside my guts.

But I'm greedy and I want the piss, too.

I turn back to the toilet bowl.

"He wants the piss, too," Dom says through pants, now patting me with a thwack on the shoulder. "Don't you, son? The pigboy wants the piss, too."

Is he gonna push my head into the bowl and make me drink the piss?

Or should I just tip forward and dipping my head inside, slurp up the piss myself, no assistance needed?

Leaning past me, Dom grabs the soggy toilet roll and pulls off the dripping paper. "Open wide," he says, but without wasting any time, he grabs my chin and shoves the soggy roll in my mouth.

"Eat it, son," he orders. "Show a bloke you respect his fuckin' generosity."

I start to chew. My jaw works up and down. Up and down. The paper is soggy and pissy and my hole feels like it's gonna drop out ... or off ... but I'm gonna chew all that fucking soggy paper and swallow it all down ... Dom is watching me.

He's making sure I chew it all up and swallow it all down.

I need to make sure I chew it all up and swallow it all down.

Chew chew chew ... swallow ... chew chew chew ... swallow ... my teeth grind against soggy pissy toilet paper ... chew chew chew ... swallow.

Piss drips from my lips and down my chin.

Chew chew chew ... and ... final ... swallow. Breathing out, I smell my pissy breath.

I wipe piss drips off my mouth and chin with the back of my hand, then lick my knuckles, tasting the very last of Mate's piss.

There's some action behind me in the semi-dark. Dom is pulling something out of his pocket. It looks like a business card. He wipes it on his cummy cock, folds it in half lengthways, then groping for my arse, probes for my hole with his finger and satisfied he's found the right spot, shoves the folded card deep inside my spent pucker.

Slapping my arse with his dirty paw, "I think we're needed somewhere else," he says. Dom and Mate pick up their cocks and moments later, after Mate bruises past me and slaps my arse too, they're gone.

Sounds of back-slapping and muscle bear bonding grow faint.

I stand up. I guess the show must be over.

Looking up at the four-guy cheer squad staring down at me from the other cubicles, I see now there's only one guy left.

"You want me to eat ya hole out, mate?" he asks.

Maybe it's not over just yet ...

He's probably about 40, I think, from what I can see in the semi-dark. He hops down from his perch.

"Clean ya up real good," he says, poking his head around the cubicle door.

He flashes a grin. Encouraged by my exhaustion – or my lack of a spoken response – he crouches down behind my arse, sitting on his haunches. Funny, he wants to eat the cum out of my fuckhole but he's not so keen on kneeling in a gritty puddle of piss.

I flinch as he fingers my hole to gingerly extract the business card. "Let me wipe it for ya," he says, and runs both sides across his tongue.

How thoughtful, I think, as he hands it to me – its letters are glow-in-the-dark!

"What does it say?" the bloke says.

Unfolding my body as I unfold the business card, I stand up straight to read aloud the words: "DOM ANON. Master Nasty Fucker."

Beneath that is printed his email address and – yes! finally! – his mobile number.

"You know, mate, a soft tongue on a wrecked hole can do ya wonders," he says.

Balding and clean-shaven, with just a bit of a gut hanging out of his loose white t-shirt, he looks so eager to please and I'm so fucking wrecked, who am I to say no?

"Sure," I say. I bend over again and grip the rim of the toilet bowl. He pulls my cheeks apart and slides his silky tongue inside my hole, gently licking, probing, sucking, felching, caressing, cajoling the hot dom cum out of me.

"Tastes good," he says, between slurps and licks and gulps. Then adds, "Jeez, yore a lucky bugga."

"Yeah?" I say. And leaning forward, I dip my hand in the toilet bowl, scooping up rank three-day-old piss, and drink.

# PARTY IN THE PUB CAR PARK

I haven't shot my load in three days. My balls are so blue they're a swollen knot inside my shorts.

It's Tuesday Truckie Night tonight at the Royal Hotel. And I know Dom aka 'DOM ANON. Master Nasty Fucker' likes to attend Tuesday Truckie Night. And ever since I was fucked, gobbed on and drank a fuckload of piss under his dom direction in the Royal Hotel toilets, I've wanted to meet up again.

Maybe even get him to buy me a real drink this time.

But he's not answering emails. And he's not answering text messages either. And fuck it! Every time I think of his pounding cock, my arsehole spasms.

I know the truckies meet out the back. Not in the beer garden. Not in the pretty, recently renovated car park with new bitumen, new white lines marking out neat parking spots, new bushes planted between every row, and candle pines surrounding three sides of the perimeter. They meet in the 'other' car park down the dark laneway.

So that's where I'm headed.

My feet quicken as I disappear into the dark.

Low voices in the distance tell me I should veer right. The 'other' car park soon appears behind a faded 'Royal Hotel car park' sign. A rusty, dented, corrugated iron fence surrounds a big square of packed dirt. No lines mark the dirt. No bushes pretty up parking spots; no candle pines surround the perimeter.

Just fence and dirt and a couple of exhausted weeds.

My hole twitches now, pulsing with the throb in my cock. They want out of my shorts, my jock, in the open air doing what they need to be doing. Where the fuck are these truckies?

A few cars – some souped up and reflective in the moonlight; some older and sadder but more practical – stand guard. And some utes, too. But no trucks.

But ... hang on ...

Towards the back of the car park, in the corner, hidden by a couple of cars, stands a circle of blokes. Some dressed in overalls and dark work shirts, or shorts and holey t-shirts, they look like truckies. Probably about ten, I count, as I walk towards them. Some hold bottles of beer, while empty ones are stacked on the ground. My shoes scuff on the dirt, making enough sound to announce my arrival, but not enough to announce it like a cough.

Closer ...

Some hold their cocks out as they piss onto a dusty pair of old workboots, set in the middle of the circle. A couple of trickles hardly splash the workboots, but there's one stream that's hitting right inside one of the boots, a big, beautiful arc of piss.

My cock bounces inside my shorts.

My arsehole winces with expectation.

A stone scutters at the end of my shoe and the truckies look up.

The truckie shooting the perfect stream looks straight at me.

Gold!

It's Dom. Hips thrust forward. Grey and yellow high-vis, short dark beard, dark close-cropped hair, big meaty paws holding his cock as he shoots piss into the boot.

"Hope I haven't caught you fellas doing something too private," I say.

"Ay, that's pigboy," says a voice beside Dom. It's Mate, the ginger muscle bear who on my last visit to the Royal, brutally face-fucked me then pissed on the toilet roll.

The toilet roll which Dom, for an encore, then shoved in my mouth.

Then watched me chew up and swallow down, every pissy, soggy morsel. Then jammed his business card inside my arse. (Though he did fold it first.)

"He's no pigboy," says another deep voice. "He's a fuckin' daddypig."

The circle chuckles.

I don't care what they fucking call me. Even in the dark Dom's a fucking man mountain: tall and built, big round pecs, massive furry arms, a confidence that towers over the other truckies in the circle. (I assume they're all truckies. Though judging by their neater clothes, some of them might be in trucking company admin.)

"You here to join us, daddypig?" another voice asks.

My cock is so hard in my shorts it's broken loose of my jock and is leaking like a bitch.

I scan the group. Bears and muscle bears – fuck, I LOVE muscle bears! – and nothing makes me want to sink to my knees faster than the prospect of a big hard throbbing dom muscle bear cock delivering deep into one of my holes.

Fuck it! I pull down my shorts, snap down my jock, pull out my cock, rub my finger across my knob, scrape up pre-cum with my finger, and stick it in my mouth.

The night air is cool on my naked arse cheeks.

Then, "Waddaya have in mind?" I ask.

I know soon enough. One of the truckies grabs me by the arm and pulls me over to a car. He bends me over the hood, and hand on the back of my head as he pushes my face into the metal, "Spread 'em," he says.

I stand with my feet spread well apart and stick out my hole.

Another hand smacks my arse hard – HARD! – so it's still ringing ten, fifteen seconds later.

But there's no point resisting, so my body sinks against the hood. It's a familiar feel. The car is an old blue late '70s Ford Fairlane. I noticed this as I approached the group. The first time I was ever fucked was in the back of one, by the dance teacher at my high school. There's enough room on the back seat to anchor your feet against the roof interior and really take a pounding cock deep in your fuckhole.

Ah, the good 'ole days ...

Hands pull up my t-shirt while other hands push down my shorts to my ankles. Boots scuff on dirt as they circle my exposed arse. Other hands grab mine and push my arms over my head, so they're reaching for the windscreen. I feel like a carcass hung in a butcher shop window.

A throbbing knob rests against my pucker.

I want that cock so bad I push back against it ... but I feel his knuckles brush against my arse as he jerks his cock. And then it explodes, shooting hot sticky ropes of cum over my arse, down my crack, up my crack, dripping over my pucker ... I'd reach around and shove the hot cum in my fuckhole with my finger but I don't want to put the bloke off his delivery. I hope he's going to shove his spent fuckstick inside my hole ... this is over too fucking soon!

But then I hear boot scuffles on the dirt, and there's a change of guard.

I seem to have arrived in the other car park just in time, as in seconds the second fucker shoots a hot load over my hole, poising his cock just outside my pucker so it feels each pulsing jet of sweet mancum. Is anyone taking a video with their phone, I wonder? Fuck, I'd love to see these fellas' faces as they bust their nut.

He wipes his cummy cock against my crack, then answers my prayer by sticking his finger inside my hole, pushing his creamy cum inside me. I grip his finger with my sphincter, wanting more fingers, three fingers, four fingers, his whole fucking meaty hand up to the knuckle –

The finger pulls out and a third truckie steps in. He's more take-control, pulling my cheeks apart, pushing his whole rod against my crack as he rubs his meat up and down, grunting as he frots against it, skin on skin, leaning into it, pushing down on my back with his rough hands – I'm sure I can smell oil and grease and brake fluid as he paws me – towering over me, whispering "Give it up, give it up, give it up" into my ear.

I want to give it up, mate, but no one's taking it!

Still, it's clear I arrived just as they were ready to bust, so at least there's that, I think, as the third truckie gives a final grunt and shoots wads of milky cum all over my back. I roll my shoulders with pleasure and reach around to feel it sticky on my skin but he pushes me down against the hood and smears the cum with his hands across my back.

As he's adding the finishing touches – there must be a glass and a half of cum on my back, and he must be signing his name with his finger, too, in elaborate cursive – I hear a trickle and then a splash on the hood near my face. I twist around and see Mate pissing a hot stream. It splashes on my lips and my nose and my cheeks, so I open my mouth and stick out my tongue. Mate must have been saving his piss all day, and it runs in forceful rivers down the metal hood, soaking into the folds of my pulled-up t-shirt, on my skin, between my stomach and chest and the metal of the car hood. I waggle my tongue and with great expertise, Mate redirects his golden stream onto my mouth. It's warm and tangy and salty and my cock almost bursts between my stomach and the hood.

Mate delivers final golden spurts at my face and head, saturating me in tasty man-piss … then stops.

A deep testosterone-fuelled voice sounds in the dark. "Any of you fuckers want last crack at this pisspig?"

It's Dom, taking command.

Silence. No takers. Clearly, I'm not to everyone's taste.

But it's Dom I want anyway.

I slowly push up against the hood and standing up, turn around to see the circle of men disbanding. Folding their cocks back inside their jocks and zipping up their trousers, trudging back to their vehicles, hands in pockets, engines turning over and cars and utes pulling out of the car park.

What the fuck is happening here?

Still with his dripping cock out, Mate grabs my shoulder and pushes me back down onto the hood. "S'not over yet," he says, and I settle down for more piss. He aims his cock at my lowered head and bursts a few warm spurts on my tongue.

But the game is over.

I push my arse out to stand up but Mate clamps his big hand on my back and pushes me down again. "Not yet," he says.

Tyres crunch on dirt and the last of the truckies pulls out of the car park. Mate releases his hand and I slowly stand up.

"Where's Dom?" I ask.

"Fucked off," Mate says, pulling his jeans up.

My balls are churning to cum, my cock is about to implode in pain and my arse feels like it needs novocaine to stop its aching. "You gonna help me get off?" I ask Mate.

"Nah, mate," Mate says. "Gotta go."

And he's off too, the ginger jumping into the old blue Fairlane, slamming it into reverse, then turning right with a squeal of tyres and tearing off down the laneway.

The only thing left is a ute in the opposite corner and an old Mazda that was probably dumped there six months ago. Even the old workboots the truckies were pissing on have been hauled away.

I peel my piss-sodden t-shirt over my stomach and pull up my jock and shorts. I could jack off behind the old Mazda – I'd probably spray the front passenger door with a geyser of cum in seconds – but somehow that's like admitting defeat.

I could get angry. Or sad. But I need to make a decision, so I kick the tyre of the old Mazda, though not too hard: I'm gonna need that foot to pedal home.

Soon I'm trudging out of the car park, and back down the dark laneway. I left my bike chained to a pole out the front of the pub, but I can't walk through the pub stinking of piss.

Turning down the side street beside the pub, I see a big rig parked on the opposite side of the street. Not the whole thing, not with the trailers attached, but just the truck. Looks like it's bright red, though it's hard to tell in the night light, with MAN in silver letters across the grille. Big headlights flash.

They flashing for me?

What do I do?

Big headlights flash again.

I stand, watching the big rig.

Headlights flash again.

Shaking my head, I continue walking up the side street, heading for my bike. Dunno what the flashing lights mean, I never learned Morse code.

A squeaking truck door sounds, followed by a yell. "Hey, son!"

Turning around, Dom hangs half out of the big rig driver's door. "Yeah?!" I yell.

He crooks his hand at me, beckoning me over.

I turn my head left and look towards the pub.

I turn my head right and look towards the dark laneway.

Then I turn my head and look straight at him.

Then I walk across the street and stand beneath the driver's door, looking up at him – tall, built, big round pecs, massive furry arms, a confidence that towers over other men.

A breeze picks up and standing in the street in my pissy t-shirt, I shiver.

But I still want that fucking beer.

"I'm thirsty," I say. "For that beer you owe me."

Dom cocks his head towards the cab's interior. "Plenty of cold beers in here," he says.

He leans over and offers me his left hand. I look up at him, right into his eyes; then at the dark interior of the cab through the open door; and then at the glint of gold on his ring finger.

"Who gave you the ring?" I ask.

"My wife," he says. "Now get in my fuckin' truck."

I look at his face. Everything tells me to turn around, walk back to my bike, and pedal home.

But I grab Dom's hand, he pulls me into his truck, and the door slams behind me.

# PRIVATE PARTY, PUBLIC PARK

Exhaust brakes sigh to a stop as Dom parks his big rig by the kerb.

It's dark, and I look out through the passenger window across the deserted parklands. There'd be some action going on out there, I know, amongst the trees and the bushes and the long grass and out in the open air. Fuckholes getting loaded. Loads flooding willing mouths. Mouths guzzling down warm piss. New relationships forged against tree trunks and park benches and grimy public toilet walls.

The rig's driver's door wheezes closed and Dom heads off across the darkened park.

I guess I'm expected to follow.

Scrambling down from the cab, I follow Dom's broad shoulders and tall frame in his grey and yellow high-vis. A light breeze picks up and I shiver, reminded I'm wearing a piss-soaked t-shirt and damp shorts and jock. But I have to admit, after three guys shot their loads across my back and arse in the Royal Hotel car park, and a fourth pissed on my face and head as I bent over the hood of an old Ford Fairlane, the last place I expected to find myself a little later was at a beat …

But say "yes" and opportunities open up …

Dom stops in mid-stride, grey rolled-up sleeves cutting across his thick biceps. The gold band on his ring finger glistens in the moonlight. We're in the middle of tall grass … well, tall-ish, up to my knees. About ten metres away I see two boots in mid-air, on the end of spread legs, and a naked arse between them rhythmically rising and falling, rising and falling, to the sound of guttural grunts and gasps.

I look at Dom's face, just as he pulls off his shirt and chucks it on the grass. My cock is rock hard. For all the cum and piss shot over me tonight, I still haven't shot my load. And my balls are aching in my jock.

Peeling off my pissy t-shirt, I throw it on the grass beside Dom's.

Dom steps in behind me and grabs my hips, pulling down my shorts and jock. He runs his hand down along my crack, between my legs, flicks my balls, teases my ball sack, collecting musky man scent, which he then sniffs deep, his fingers stuck under his nostrils. Then runs his fingers under my nose and I sniff my own man funk. Then he pushes two fingers past my lips and I lick them, take them deep into my mouth, desperate for every last drop of sweat and leftover truckie cum and piss and arse juice and –

Dom's whisper is gruff in my ear. "Bend over."

I bend over, stick my arse out, and hoping by some miracle there's enough leftover truckie cum nestled in my crack to lube my arse, wait for his thick cock.

Night breeze caresses my exposed arse cheeks.

I'm waiting …

… maybe he'll shove his business card inside my hole again, like he did after our first encounter.

… but then I feel something moist and gentle on my hole, licking and kissing and nipping. Head down, I look through my legs to see who's rimming me … and to my surprise I see Dom's legs – grey work trousers pulled down so I can see his hard cock bobbing in the moonlight – and naked stomach.

He's quick on the job, and I moan as his tongue, now more insistent, throbs deeper inside my arsehole, chews on my arse lips, teeth rasping around my pucker.

"Fuck, you gotta great cunt, son," he says, his breath warm on my hole.

"Thanks," I say. I'm not a great fan of feminising my fucktools but as Dom has his tongue in my arse, I'm not gonna rock the boat too much.

And his tongue and lips certainly know their way around a manhole. He must have undertaken hours of training and tuition.

"Sloppy and open but tight when it needs to be fucked," he adds. "Tighten it."

I tighten my sphincter around his tongue ... which drives it deeper, harder inside me.

"Good boy," he says.

He bites me on the arse and I gasp, so he slaps it hard. "I could eat your fuckin' hole all night," he says.

"Please do," I whisper.

He prods it with a finger, filling my cavity, sliding it in deep ... deep ... slap up against the knuckle. I push back against it, wanting it deeper, wish his finger was longer and fatter and musclier, pistoning into me, filling my fuckhole ... fuck the finger! What I really want inside me is his cock!

Dom grabs my hips and pulls me against his mouth, spreading my hole apart with his meaty paws and reaching right up inside me with his wet, silky, probing tongue. He's such a hungry fucker, he wants to open my hole wide and long and get inside my cavernous fucking gape. And I want as much of him inside me ... nah, I NEED as much of him inside me as I can get.

The breeze kicks up and I breathe in dried piss stink on my chest. My head shakes in disbelief but acknowledgement ... the last thing I expected from Dom Anon, Master Nasty Fucker, was an expert, breathtaking rim job. Maybe that's what he's a master of ... ?

Tongue deep inside me, I look up and see a tall bloke, early 40s maybe (hard to tell in the dark) stepping towards me across the grass. T-shirt pulled behind his neck so I can see his hairy chest, his long, slightly stiff cock swings in the breeze. I look across to where the couple were rutting nearby and see the younger bottom lying back on his elbows, blond head craning above the knee-high grass, watching his Top approach me.

The Top stands in front of me, cock swaying. I breathe in, smell arse juice and sweet cum on his cockhead.

"Fuck his face," Dom orders.

I open my mouth and the Top's cock slides in. Sweaty arse and spent cum and rhythmic rutting is what I taste on my tongue. My lips clamp around his knob, tongue lashes around the head, flicking it, skimming across the piss slit, working it over. Fuck! I wish piss was gushing out of it …

The Top clasps my head and pushes his cock to the back of my throat. Girding myself, I clamp my feet to the ground and centre my body as the Top works his cock in my mouth and Dom continues to work his tongue in my arse.

You know, I still haven't cum. It's been three days since I came and that's why I pedalled to the Royal Hotel this evening, to dump a load. My sprog's backed up inside me and I'm panting for release.

My hand grabs my rock-hard cock and starts to jerk.

"Yeah, pull yourself off, son," Dom says, standing up, holding my hips. "Fuckin' jerk your meat and shoot all over his fuckin' feet."

Well, I'd be happy to oblige, I think, and may be able to after all, given the three days of pressure … but what about you, Dom, I think – when (and where) are you going to cum?

The Top pulls out of my mouth – his cock is soft, and I've licked it clean, anyway – so he stands back.

No point bending over with nothing inside me to keep me down, so I stand up. Dom reaches around and grabs my cock with his meaty paw, starts furiously jerking it, drawing into me, pushing his own hard thick meat between my legs.

My cock strains under his hand, straining to cum, straining to shoot three days of pent-up manjuice.

Dom nuzzles into my neck, biting it, teeth scraping my skin. I gasp, arch my back, push my arse against his pelvis. He reaches through my legs with his other hand and pulls on my balls, yanking them down hard, stretching the skin.

The blond-headed bottom approaches, naked except for his boots.

I feel a rush in my cock. And I fucking love an audience.

The blond watches, head cocked. I smirk. Dom releases his grip on my balls momentarily ... then yanks them down even harder. Jerks my cock with Hard. Grinding. Strokes.

I groan, a cry from my guts. Shoulders cave and spine contracts. My pelvis locks and squeezes Dom's meat between my thighs.

My cock thrusts out against Dom's grip and shudders and splutters and shoots ... shoots ... shoots ... ropes of cum into the night air ... wave after wave of three days' worth of hot creamy fuckjuice.

Cum splashes the Top's cock, his balls, his hairy thighs. My body shudders and shakes and shivers to a spent halt.

The blond drops to his knees, gobbling my cock into his mouth. I wince at the shock of his tongue, so he changes tack, now caressing, tasting, sucking, cleaning up my cock.

Dom swings his hips backward then groaning, drives his fuckstick between the grip of my thighs. Grasping my hips, he pumps his own fuckjuice into the night air, some hitting the blond's face, some shooting down my leg, all hot and sticky and sweet.

Dom bites me hard on the neck, then licks my ear, his breath hot and heavy. "Your cunt is now officially mine, son."

Oh, I think. Good to know. (Although, he kind of already claimed it in the Royal Hotel toilets ...)

The blond dips his head and starts snacking on Dom's cock, tongue licking, caressing, lapping, harvesting any leftover cum.

Dom pulls his cock away from the blond's tongue and from between my thighs, and shoves the blond on the shoulder. "On your back, fucker," he says. The blond falls back onto the grass, his boots flailing in the air, quivering, expectant.

Dom stands over him and points his cock at his chest, throws his head back and grunting, releases a hot stream of steaming piss. The blond wriggles under the stream, opens his mouth to drink. The Top takes the cue and standing beside Dom, points his own cock at the blond and hits his chest with his own stream of piss.

Dom looks at me. Do I lie next to the blond and open my mouth, too?

I grab my cock and standing with my feet apart, relax. A warm rush of piss flows out of my cock and arcs across the blond's face just as Dom's piss splutters to a stop.

The blond squirms and giggles, enjoying the piss of three exhausted men, running his hands across his skin, licking his fingers, scooping up the pooling gold with his hands and slurping it down.

Dom shakes his cock and pushes it back into his jocks. Seconds later, pulling on his grey and yellow high-vis shirt, I watch broad shoulders on a tall frame stepping across the parklands, back to his rig.

The rig brakes to a stop, engine thrumming.

Good, my bike's still chained to a light pole outside the darkened Royal Hotel.

Inside the truck cab, Dom leans towards me. Is he going to … kiss me?

I lean towards him.

Dom puckers his lips – *Ptui!* – and spits in my face.

The gob slides down my cheek. My tongue flicks out of the side of my mouth but collects nothing. Dom swipes his fingers across my face and pushes the gob in my mouth. I lick his fingers, and he wipes the sticky wet on my other cheek.

"You look like the first bloke I ever fucked," Dom whispers.

My head nods. Maybe that explains something.

Dom leans in again. I brace my face for more gob on my other cheek, my nose, my eyelids, my mouth … but he sticks his tongue out and pushes my head down.

"He was my soccer coach," he murmurs.

And licks my forehead.

My shoulders shrug. Maybe it explains nothing.

Hands resting back on the steering wheel, the ring on his left hand glints in the streetlight.

"Where'd you get the ring?" I ask.

He presses a button on the dash and the passenger door opens. "Get outta my fuckin' truck."

I scramble down out of the truck, and as he lowers the driver's window, nip around the cab to the driver's side. Standing in the deserted street in my still pissy t-shirt, I shiver.

Dom nods towards the pub. "I'm here every Tuesday night, son. See you next Tuesday."

The window rolls up, the engine grinds into gear, and the big rig slowly pulls away into the night.

# SAUNA SLING PARTY

Last time we met he slapped my arse then clamping his big hand on my back, forced me down onto the hood of his Ford Fairlane.

Then shot a hot arc of salty piss on my face and tongue.

(I know him because he usually plays second fiddle to Dom the Master Nasty Fucker.)

But here he stands at the end of the passageway, arms folded across his chest, thick cock tenting the standard-issue white towel. The wall sconce above highlights his ginger hair cropped so close it's almost a skull cap. There's a similar spray dusting his pecs, and as I step closer, I see the flash of metal through his round, very erect, very pale pink nipples. My mouth is already watering.

I look down at the tent in his towel. 'Mate,' I want to say, for that's what I call him in my head. Dunno what his real name is, though – Ginger? Blue? Fred?

(Probably Adrian!)

He leers at me, but it's a friendly leer. I think he recognises me, remembers me from the Royal Hotel car park bent over his Fairlane, maybe even from the hot piss-and-fuck threesome we'd had a few weeks before that in the hotel toilets.

He nods, looks down at his looming pole, back at my eyes. His tongue is working inside his mouth. Is he going to gob in my face?

Lifting my towel slightly, I scratch under my balls. My cock hardens at the thought of his spit sticky on my cheeks.

Mate unfolds his arms and grabbing my bicep, pulls me along the passageway. Sliding open a door, he grips my shoulder then pushes me inside a cubicle.

In the dim light I see a black sling hanging from the ceiling.

Closing the door behind him – but not latching it shut – he throws his towel into a corner as my towel drops to the floor. Perching my arse on the edge of the sling, I grab the chains that snake up to the ceiling, slide my arse backward, then relax against the rubber. Spreading my legs, I hook my feet around the chains, then grab the other chains above my shoulders with my hands and leaning back, concentrate on loosening my hole.

I'm hoping it's gonna get a servicing.

Mate squats beside my open legs and starts into it, first fingertips then knuckles against my manhole, and then ... dips in with his – oh! – velvety tongue.

My body shudders with pleasure and my cock slaps hard against my stomach as his tongue caresses my hole. His mouth snacks on it, licks it, bites it, nips it, gnaws it. He pushes his fingers inside past the first – second – as far as the third knuckle with one ... then two ... then three then ... four ... fingers. He stares at it as he works, eyes boring into my cavity, gazing deep inside my gape, showering my manhole with the attention it deserves, giving it the workout a dom Top demands is his fucking right.

He grabs my hips and pulls me towards his face. My legs untwine from the chains above, my knees drop onto my chest, and my hole opens wider for deeper access.

My hole now slick with his saliva, Mate stands up, spits on it – *ptui!* – then looks in my eyes, grabs my throbbing cock with one hand, pulls my balls down hard with the other so I arch my back in pain and pleasure – ooooh! – then launches another phlegmy gob – *ptui!* – smack between my nipples.

The door slides open, and a muscle bear steps inside. Tall, dark hair on his head and chest, his towel slides down to reveal a thick girthy meatstick and heavy balls swinging between his muscly legs. He latches the door closed behind him and slaps Mate on his arse, then wrapping his arm around Mate's shoulders, pulls into him and sniffs his face, a slow, lingering huff. Mate drops his grip on my tackle and opens his mouth, his nipple piercings a brief glint in the dim light as the muscle bear slips his tongue inside.

"Mmm," the muscle bear hums. "Tasty hole juice."

Muscle bear smiles at me. Hip rubbing against my side, he reaches across and grabs my nipples. His fingertips are rough, like sandpaper, workman tradie fingers, hard and coarse and callused and he runs them across my nipple tips. I gasp, abdominal muscles contracting as his fingers send hot shocks through me. My mouth wide and my eyes wider, Mate spies his chance and slides his throbbing cockhead into my open arse. I hold my breath, waiting for his cock to dig deep inside my trench.

Mate's cock doesn't disappoint. Pulling out just a little, he squirts lube on his shaft, then pushes his fuckstick in to the hilt, his thick meat opening me up, plunging deep inside my guts. And he starts to rock, hips thrusting into me, working a steady rhythm. His meaty paws grip my thighs and as he shoves his pole into me I grunt, pushing against his groin as I want more of his meatstick deep deep deep inside me.

The muscle bear doesn't disappoint either. Standing behind my head, he reaches forward to pinch my nipples between his index fingers and thumbs, pulling them hard as Mate's cock works my hole, in and out. As I rock back and forth off Mate's pelvis, his cock slamming into me, through my arselips then back inside me again and out and in and past my arselips and driving deep inside again and again and opening my fuckhole more and deeper and longer and wider and sharper, muscle bear pinches my nipples between his fingernails. Shards of exquisite pain shoot through my chest and heart and head with each tug, each rock, each thrust, each jab. And I moan and gasp and gulp and rasp, my nipples pulling with each squeeze of muscle bear's fingers and each ram of Mate's muscly meatpole.

I throw my head back in the sling, stretching my body out to make more arse-enlightening fuckspace for Mate's pile-driving cock, stretching each extreme nipple squeeze just that stinging millimetre more.

Mate grunts. Then groans, louder, hands like a vice around my thighs. He stares into my face, his cock buried inside my guts, his nuts so tight against my sloppy hole they're half inside me.

Muscle bear pushes into my nipples, grinding them into my pecs. I cry out, loud, in pain, just as Mate's eyes roll back into his head and thrusting forward, he shoots into my hole. And just as muscle bear's hands release my nips I feel the pulse of Mate's cock against my ring as he spasms into me … pumps his hot jizz into me … pumps … and pumps … and shoots … and growls …

I cough, my spasming stomach wrenching my hole away from Mate's spent meat. His cock slips out with a slurp, and I look up into muscle bear's face as he peers over me, asking him, what's next?

As Mate steps back, muscle bear nips around to access my spread legs and taking charge, plunges his fingers deep inside my trembling gape. He pulls them out, runs his tongue along a finger, licks Mate's cum and my arse juice off it, then pushes his hand in front of my face and offers me the rest. I open my lips as he shoves all his fingers in my mouth. Man cum and arse juice and Mate's spit and a hint of lube slide across my tongue and I savour their funky sweaty sleazy taste. I grab his hand and scrape every drop off his rough fingers with my teeth, lingering with the probing touch of my tongue.

Mate has already picked up his towel, and after slapping me on the arse, he unlatches the door and slides it open. Peering around muscle bear, I see other guys are standing outside the cubicle, listening, hoping to join the action. Two slip inside the cubicle as muscle bear bends close to my ear.

"I'm gonna hit the showers," he says. "But I'll be back for round two."

# SOUNDS OF PLEASURE, SOUNDS OF PAIN

I have a soft spot for rangas (aka bloodnuts or gingers). And so when I realise it's actually 'Mate' online, I can't resist.

We have met before.

He pissed on a roll of toilet paper in the Royal Hotel toilets then made me chew the pissy paper down.

Later, he pissed on me while I was spread across the bonnet of his Ford Fairlane in the Royal Hotel car park.

And on our third encounter he and a fuckbuddy fucked me in the sling at the sauna.

His skin is pale and he's built and bearish. And while I call him 'Mate' in my head, as I first encountered him in a shaming threesome with Dom the Master Nasty Fucker, I also have this weird feeling his real name is Adrian.

So we have a history. But I want to take it further, to another level. And Mate wants to, too.

I chain my cycle to the railings of the fence outside his front door. He lives in a townhouse in a leafy inner-city suburb, not far from my ex-psychiatrist and recent fuck Gareth's consulting rooms, and as I knock on the door at 8.00pm as planned, wonder what other secrets Mate holds.

The door flies open. Mate stands dressed in a white towel. His ginger hair is cropped so close it's almost a skull cap. There's a similar fuzz across his pecs, and a flash of metal through his round, very erect, very pale pink nipples.

I step inside the tiled entry hall, the door closes behind me, his towel drops to the floor and I drop, too. The tiles are cold and hard on my knees. He pushes his meaty cock with its trimmed ginger pubes in my face. My natural response is to open my mouth, and he pushes his cockhead in so it sits on my tongue. I taste … lube, and … disinfectant?

He pulls his cock out of my mouth and says, "Daddypig, I've started already."

Picking up the towel from the floor, he disappears into the living room. I stand up and follow. An office chair sits in the middle of the floor. Beside it stands a coffee table with another white towel laying across it. And on the towel sit a tube of lube, a bottle of disinfectant, and a variety of thin metal rods, some with bumps and ridges, others sleek and smooth, all sexily serious, meaning business.

Mate throws his towel on the office chair and slumps into it, legs spread, balls hanging low, cock half hard. As I pull off my t-shirt and cycle shorts, my cock and knackers bounce free. Except my knackers are bound with white cord, tied up and separated so they stand tight and proud, shiny and expectant, ready for play.

Mate leers at my balls with interest. Leaning forward, he reaches out and fondles them, holds them, bends and sticks his tongue out, licks them, sucks them, before pulling away and grabbing them hard, cramping them together. I hum in appreciation. And then I moan as he taps them, not hard, but enough for me to feel the force of his hand up and under my stomach.

"Nice boys," he says, "You're treating them well."

This is the most I've ever heard him communicate to me, I think, so in celebration I take a chance and fall to my knees onto hard tiles again, start fondling, rolling his balls in my hands, feeling their weight on my fingers, enjoying their heft.

As I hold them he picks up a metal sound, flicks open the lube and slathers lube down the sound's shaft. The sound is long and shiny, no bumps or ridges.

"Grip 'em," he instructs.

I grip his balls and he poises the sound outside his piss slit. He looks at me, then back at his piss slit, slowly pushes the metal rod into the opening. Stop. Then holding his cock perfectly vertical and the sound perfectly straight above it, pushes it in a little further. He breathes, looks at me, half-grimace and half-grin. Then presses his cockhead to open the piss slit more, and the sound slides in just a little, just a little bit more, just a little more again, lube globbing at the opening.

Mate breathes out, slowly jerks his cock. "Squeeze 'em," he says, so I squeeze his nuts harder and he gasps, we both gasp, but his is louder.

The metal sound rides up his piss tube so he pushes it back down again, slowly, carefully, but with a stoic look on his face, breathes out, looks me in the eyes, back at the metal sound riding his piss tube, back at me, then takes his hand off the sound.

"Go on," he says.

I release my grip on his balls, and holding his hard cock in one hand, tap the blunt top of the sound with my other index finger. Just lightly. Mate breathes out. Then I tap it again, and again, and again, slowly pushing it down with each tap, with each breath Mate utters, with each breath I take.

I've sounded before. But only alone. With a set I bought. A variety of metal rods with bauble studs increasing in diameter up the sound, with smoothed ridges along its shaft, with a larger flared diameter halfway along, with rings and knobs at the very top for easy gripping. And silicon snakes too, much longer, various thicknesses, to really get down deep inside your urethra, where you can really really feel it behind your balls, under your stomach. It's an amazing feeling – painful and pleasurable and I think it's hot (I think) but for me, while I sounded more than a few times, I realised I needed something more. It was hot … but alone, it wasn't hot enough!

Mate's cock is hard hard hard. His breathing is heavy and I know he feels pain but I also know how much pleasure he's feeling, too. The sound rises a little, like his cock is rejecting it.

"You want another sound?" I ask him.

206

He shakes his head. "This is the best."

His cock is red and straining and his face is flushed and grim and his eyes hazy and half-lidded but it's so so so fucking hot. My own cock is rock hard and my bound balls are tight tight tight as I push the sound further down Mate's piss tube, and he groans as it descends, me holding his cock again as he's lost in the pleasure and pain.

I take a chance. Still on my knees, I tap the top of the sound, sending little waves of shock, of tension, of sensation through Mate's body, I reach under his balls and tap them too, two taps, enough for his boys to really feel it.

"Aaargh!" he says.

I wait before continuing.

"Fuckin' again!" he says.

So I tap his balls again, twice, and again, and again, tap tap, tap tap, tap tap, tap tap, as he now works the sound up and down his piss tube and slowly jerks his meat at the same time.

I know that feeling – it is exquisite. It's another plane. It's almost astral.

The sound pops up and it looks dry, so I grab the lube and squirt some more on the sound and Mate works it back down into his piss tube again, a big sigh and a groan and he grabs his cock and jerks it again.

"Pull 'em, squeeze 'em," he says, so I grip his nuts again and pull them as he grips his cock and jerks it and slowly works the sound up and down, up and down, up and up and then dow-own and up and up then dow-own and up and up then dow-own and faster with his jerking and grunting and I'm holding his balls, gripping them, pulling them, and he's pushing the sound down as it rides up and his jerking grows faster faster faster and he growls as the metal rod rises again and he pushes it back down and gasps and tenses his stomach and his shoulders cave and he grunts and jerks and growls and he cries out and the sound pops up and he pulls it out and it clangs on the floor as his cock erupts, shoots cum out of his cock and up over his cockhead and down the shaft and splashes runs streams thick and juicy down over his ballsack and my hand gripping his knackers and over his pubes and more hot white sticky jets of cum dripping chugging jetting from his piss slit and he shudders and more cum pumps and he must he must have been saving this for a week. Fuck, it's everywhere and his cock looks red spent exhausted.

I scrape cum up with my fingers and stick them in my mouth, licking it down. There's so much it's a feast. Scrape more off his cock and ballsack and sprouting ranga pubes and eat it lick it suck sticky hot thick mancream down my gullet, still on my knees, my balls still bound tight with white cord, jutting out ripe ready for plucking, my cock hard, my nipples erect.

"Stand up," Mate says.

So I stand up.

Mate reaches over and grabs my nuts, then pulls. The pull, the stretch, the squeeze has me craving more. I gasp.

Leaning forward, he opens his mouth and looks up at me. "Gimme your fuckin' cum," he says.

And pulling my balls again, pushes his lips over my cock and twists his tongue around my knob. I breathe out, grab his head with both hands, and relax as he sets to work milking me like the cocksucking expert he so clearly is.

www.ingramcontent.com/pod-product-compliance
Lightning Source LLC
Chambersburg PA
CBHW031950010726
47493CB00007B/2153